A House
Full of
Strangers

A HOUSE
FULL OF
STRANGERS

Emily Rhoads Johnson

COBBLEHILL BOOKS/DUTTON

New York

"To Look at Any Thing" from THE LIVING SEED, copyright © 1962 by
John Moffitt and renewed 1990 by Henry K. Moffitt, reprinted by permission
of Harcourt Brace Jovanovich, Inc.

Library of Congress Cataloging-in-Publication Data
Johnson, Emily Rhoads.
A house full of strangers / Emily Rhoads Johnson.
p.   cm.
Summary: Flora, a young naturalist, finds solace in the woods near her
home following the death of her grandmother and the arrival of a large,
noisy family of relatives.
ISBN 0-525-65091-1
[1. Family life—Fiction. 2. Nature—Fiction. 3. Trees—Fiction.
4. Forests and forestry—Fiction.] I. Title.
PZ7.J631758Ho 1992   [Fic]—dc20   91-41104   CIP   AC

Published in the United States by Cobblehill Books,
an affiliate of Dutton Children's Books,
a division of Penguin Books USA Inc.,
375 Hudson Street, New York, New York 10014
Designed by Joy Taylor
Printed in the United States of America
First Edition   10 9 8 7 6 5 4 3 2 1

To Glenn and Heidi,

and in memory of my sister,
Hester Rhoads Bradbury,
who understood the language of trees

Contents

viii

A House
Full of
Strangers

ONE

The Take-Over

FLORA was halfway up the stairs when she heard the rattley-bang of an old pickup pulling into the driveway. The sound sent a shiver of dread up her backbone. Pressed into a corner of the landing, she wondered if this was how an animal felt when it was trapped, awaiting capture.

From where she stood, Flora had a clear view of the front hallway. Everything in it was so familiar that she could have pictured it with her eyes closed: the glazed umbrella stand, the letter basket, the drop-leaf table with its round lace doily, and the old coat rack with Gram's plaid raincoat still draped over one hook. Through the archway to the living room she caught glimpses of Miss Kimball hurriedly plumping pillows, straightening curtains, blowing dust off the furniture. Miss Kimball was the social worker who had picked Flora up at the foster home this morning and brought her back here. All she'd talked about the whole way over was how lucky Flora was to have a family coming all the way from Kentucky to take care of her.

But what Miss Kimball didn't understand was that Flora didn't *want* a family. She had tried to convince her, just as she'd tried to convince the judge at the courthouse, that she was perfectly capable of taking care of herself. But all along she knew it was no use. No grown-up was going to allow an eleven-year-old girl to live in a house by herself—even the house she had lived in her whole life.

It was too late now to change their minds. Now nothing would ever be the same. Not ever.

The door burst open, and suddenly the whole house exploded with running feet and high-pitched voices.

"Hey, wow! Are we really gonna live here?"

"Hey look, Ma, a fireplace!"

"I get first dibs on bedrooms!"

"Do not!"

"Do too!"

Watching from her corner on the landing, Flora saw a thin, tired-looking woman take Miss Kimball's hand, then turn to the man beside her and exclaim, "Isn't this the loveliest house, Walter? It's just what we've always dreamed of!"

But the man wasn't listening. He was too busy trying to grab all the children at once as they slipped from his grasp and spread in every direction like ants over a picnic table. Some of them disappeared into the kitchen where Flora heard cupboard doors bang open and shut. A squabble broke out and someone started to howl.

Flora felt as if she were observing a play in the school auditorium. Surely this was make-believe. It *had* to be. It couldn't be real. This band of aliens couldn't really be moving in here, turning the house that had been hers and Gram's into some kind of amusement park!

But Gram was gone. Flora knew *that* was real because she was the one who had found her curled up on the sofa three weeks ago with the rose-colored afghan pulled up to her chin. She had looked so peaceful there, as if she were sleeping. But Flora had known, even before she touched the cold blue fingers clutching the afghan, that her grandmother's eyes would not open again.

A tiny girl clutching a Popsicle in one hand toddled unsteadily toward the stairway. It was April and unusually warm even for southern Indiana, so the sticky pink ice was melting fast and leaving a trail of drips on the floor.

"What do you think you're doin', Pollyann?" An older girl with dark smudges where her eyes should have been rushed at the child with a handful of paper towels. "You shouldn't be eatin' that thing in here. Now go in the kitchen with Curtis while I clean up this mess."

Another girl wearing a striped sunsuit and oversized cowboy boots was hopping up and down like a small kangaroo, tugging at the woman's elbow. "Let's go upstairs, Mama," she pleaded. "I wanna see the bedrooms."

Flora froze. They were coming up. She pressed herself even harder against the wall in a desperate attempt to become invisible.

"Oh!" The woman stopped in front of Flora and smiled. "You must be Flora. I didn't see you standing here so quiet."

She extended her free hand and Flora clasped it cautiously.

"I'm Abbie Quigg," the woman said. Her dress was rumpled

from the long drive, and her hair fell in limp strands around her face. "You can call me 'Aunt Abbie' if you like," she said, laughing, "—because in a way I guess that's what I am."

She introduced the child at her side. "This is Missy—the young'un who couldn't sit still if her life depended on it."

The girl, who looked about seven, peered up at Flora with eyes as big as washtubs. "Is there a bathroom up there?" she demanded.

Abbie shrugged an apology and hustled the child up the stairs.

THE ODD THING was, until her grandmother died, Flora hadn't known she *had* relatives. Of course, the Quiggs weren't full-blooded relatives, Miss Kimball had explained to her, but more like *half*-relatives because Flora's mother was Abbie Quigg's half-sister. It was all so complicated and overwhelming that Flora hadn't even tried to figure it out. All she knew was that Gram had willed her house to the Quiggs on the condition that they live in it and take care of Flora until her eighteenth birthday.

Miss Kimball came to the foot of the stairs and smiled up at Flora. "So *there* you are!" she exclaimed brightly. "I've been looking for you, dear. Come on down and meet the rest of the Quiggs." The way she said it made Flora feel like a cat being coaxed out of a tree.

Gripping the oak banister with one hand, Flora crept slowly down the stairs. With every step she felt herself moving deeper and deeper into a long dark tunnel without any end.

A heavyset man with gentle eyes and a stubble of beard strode out of the kitchen and thrust a hand toward her.

"Howdy, Flora," he said, "I'm Walter Quigg. We were awful sorry to hear about your grandma. Abbie and me, we never had the good fortune to meet 'er, but we've heard she was a mighty special lady. I know you'll be missin' her."

Flora stared past the man's shoulder and fixed her eyes on Gram's raincoat. Tears welled up, but she forced them back. She would not cry. Not in front of strangers.

"This here's Curtis," Mr. Quigg went on, waving toward a chunky boy in the kitchen doorway who was dabbing at his nose with a Kleenex. "The weeds out here in the country are makin' his allergies kick up. But he'll be better soon's we find a doc in town to give him his shots."

Curtis Quigg appeared to be about ten and had a sullen, unhealthy look about him. He stopped dabbing long enough to narrow his watery eyes at Flora. "You the girl who comes with the house?" he snuffled.

"Curtis John," his father reprimanded him, "you keep a civil tongue in your head, y'hear? Gettin' this house is the best thing ever happened to us, and you're lucky to have a nice new cousin come along with it."

Flora turned away and looked into the living room where the girl with the smudged eyes was draped like a dead fish over Gram's favorite chair.

"That's Doreen," Mr. Quigg informed her, following her gaze. "She's fifteen goin' on twenty-five and spends most of her time wrestlin' with her hair." He winked at Flora as if he were letting her in on a family joke.

Doreen's hair did look like something that had recently fought in a wrestling match and lost, observed Flora. It stood out from her head like a cloud of dry yellow seaweed. And the smudges around her eyes, Flora could see now, were from

5

makeup that seemed to have been applied with a caulking gun.

"Hi." Doreen smiled and gave Flora a little wave like a parade queen waving from a convertible.

Not knowing what else to do, Flora waved back.

Doreen raised her long lashes questioningly. "Where's your TV?" she inquired. "I don't see one anywhere."

"Oh . . . uh, we don't have a TV." Flora felt flustered. "I mean, we don't have one down here. It's upstairs—in a closet."

"In a *closet*?" Doreen's face squinched up like she'd bitten a lemon.

"My grandmother hated television," Flora explained. "She only brought it out when I had to watch something for school."

"Oh." Doreen seemed to have a hard time taking this in. Finally she said, "Well then, it's a good thing we brought our own."

TWO

The China Cup

BACK IN Kentucky the Quiggs had lived in a furnished duplex, so all they'd brought with them to Indiana were clothes and bedding and dishes—plus two television sets. The bigger one went into the living room in front of the bookcase, and the smaller one on the kitchen counter. As soon as the sets were plugged in, someone turned them both on. And they stayed on all day, although everybody was too busy getting settled in to watch them. It was as if this family couldn't exist without constant noise, thought Flora. As if a little peace and quiet might be more than they could handle.

THE NEXT morning when she passed her grandmother's bedroom, Flora's face flushed with anger when she saw her aunt kneeling in front of Gram's dresser, lifting nightgowns and sweaters out of the drawers and placing them in cardboard boxes. Taking a few timid steps into the room, she asked, "What are you doing with Gram's clothes, Aunt Abbie?" Her throat was so tight that her voice squeaked.

"Oh, Flora, you startled me!" Abbie looked up, her face flustered. "I was hopin' to have these things packed away by the time you got up."

"Why?" asked Flora. "What are you going to do with them?"

"Just pack them in boxes for now," she replied, "to make room in these drawers for our clothes—Walter's and mine. We'll put your grandma's clothes in the attic until—well, until you're more used to the idea of her bein' gone. Later maybe you can help us decide what to do with 'em—who to give 'em to."

Flora stepped further into the room—the room that had always offered her such comfort, such peace. For a moment she just stood there staring at the faded nightgowns heaped forlornly in an old cardboard box. Suddenly she couldn't bear the thought of all Gram's things being locked away in the attic where she would never see them. She glanced at the lavender sweater Abbie was folding. "Couldn't I—" she burst out, "I mean, do you think I might keep out a few of Gram's things —to remember her by?"

Abbie stood up. "Well *sure*, honey, that's a *fine* idea. You just come over here and anything you see you want to keep, you set it right there on the bed."

After deliberating a moment, Flora chose a white cotton blouse that a friend of her grandmother's had sent her from Germany. Flora had always loved the green tassels at the neck and the bright-winged birds and flowers embroidered on the yoke. The other things she chose were small enough to tuck into a shoebox: an inlaid marble box Gram said came from the Taj Mahal in India; the pearl-drop earrings she always wore when she went out to dinner or to programs at Flora's school; the china thimble and the little scissors shaped like a stork from her sewing basket. She hung the blouse on a hanger in her closet and tucked the shoebox on the highest shelf.

FLORA was the last one to the breakfast table that morning. No one noticed her except Uncle Walter, who smiled pleasantly and passed her the almost empty platter of pancakes. Flora took one and put it on her plate. "Would someone please pass the syrup?" she asked.

Of course no one heard her. Pollyann was gurgling like a frog and rubbing butter in her hair. Missy was wrestling the syrup pitcher away from Curtis who called her a "Pighead" while syrup dribbled figure eights across the tablecloth. Doreen was staring sulkily at the newspaper hiding her father's face and whining, "*Please* let me get new jeans for school, Daddy? *Pleeeeze?*"

Flora felt like screaming. Could this really be the same kitchen where every day for six years she and Gram had eaten all their meals together, chatting and laughing, or sometimes just listening to the birds in the trees outside?

Closing her eyes, she took a deep breath the way Gram had taught her to do whenever she was about to explode. Carefully she lifted the big china teacup filled with cambric tea and held it in both hands. Just holding it and feeling the warmth of the hot tea-and-milk helped her forget that Gram wasn't here, that these strangers hadn't really invaded her world, making her feel like an unwelcome guest in her own house.

9

With her eyes, Flora followed the gold design that circled the cup's rim, then let her gaze rest on one of the purple violets with heart-shaped leaves that wound around the sides. There was even a small bud painted inside the bottom of the cup that stayed hidden until the very last swallow. Flora set the cup on its saucer and was picking up her fork when suddenly the syrup pitcher flew out of Missy's hand and crashed down on the teacup, smashing it to smithereens.

Flora gasped. At first all she could do was hold her breath and stare in horror at the broken china strewn across her uneaten pancake. Leaping from her chair, she whirled on Missy.

"You broke it!" she yelled at her. "You broke our special cup! Gram's grandmother gave her that cup when she was twelve years old and she drank out of it every day and was going to give it to me on my twelfth birthday!" Breathing hard, she glared at the wispy-haired girl whose chin had begun to tremble. "You're clumsy and stupid and I *hate* you! I hate you all! I wish you'd never come here! You've ruined everything!"

Never in her whole life had Flora ever yelled at anyone. She didn't know what had come over her. It was as if someone else's voice—not Flora Mae Haywood's—had come out of her mouth. Tears started down her face, and she bolted for the door.

When her uncle called her back she hesitated, then overheard her aunt say, "Let 'er be, Walter. It hasn't been easy for her. Maybe she needs to be by herself for a bit."

Abbie's words brought a fresh flood of tears burning down Flora's cheeks, and she ran blindly through the backyard and into the woods behind the big yellow house. Twigs and brambles lashed at her face, but she didn't care. All she wanted was to get away.

The path wove in and out among beech trees and sycamores, dogwoods and maples. It was late April, and masses of white anemones carpeted the forest floor like drifts of snow. Here and there yellow violets were springing up alongside the trillium and bellflowers and Dutchman's-breeches. Flora knew the name of every flower in the woods, but today they meant nothing to her.

Today felt like the end of the world.

FLORA knew of only one place to run—to her tree, a huge maple at the far end of the woods. She and Gram were the only ones who knew the way to the tree; and Flora was thankful now that the path was vague and winding because she didn't want any of those stupid half-cousins, or whatever they were, following her to her secret place. First she had to find her way to the only place in the creek shallow enough to cross. After leaping from rock to rock across the water, she wove her way along the path until she reached the old oak tree riddled with woodpecker holes that was one of her landmarks. She stopped for a moment to catch her breath, then continued on, winding around tree trunks and ducking under branches as nimbly as a young deer.

This was her world. Now it was her only refuge.

Flora's tree was a large, stately maple that stood by itself at the edge of a clearing that had once been a farmyard. It was fuller than the other trees in the woods because it had more space around it, and more sunlight in which to grow. Breathless from her run through the forest, Flora threw her arms around the tree's thick trunk and nuzzled the bark with her cheek. Then, grasping the lowest branch with both hands, she walked her sneakered feet up the trunk and hoisted herself into the tree.

Where the main trunk forked in a Y, a third branch jutted out like an elbow, almost parallel with the ground. Flora settled herself into the crotch of this three-armed Y as cozily as a squirrel curling up in its nest. Instantly a familiar peacefulness took hold of her. She leaned back, closed her eyes, and breathed in the sweet earthy fragrance rising softly around her.

Wrapped in her tree's sturdy arms, nothing could harm her.

Six years ago, on a morning like this one, she and her mother had been exploring the deserted farm that was part of her grandmother's property. Flora remembered how the tree had actually seemed to stretch toward her, inviting her to climb into its branches. Her mother had laughed, then lifted her up to the first branch where she had sat in wonder, gazing down at the grass and the flowers and her mother's glistening hair.

SUDDENLY Flora heard something—a voice so faint, it was like an echo. She covered her ears with her hands to drown out the sound. It was *them* . . . calling her name . . . trying to find her. She pressed herself tighter against the tree, wishing for a door in the trunk so she could slip inside. Then the calling stopped. She uncovered her ears to listen. Nothing. Then a different sound—short explosive chuffs followed by a long wheeze. The school bus was leaving without her!

So what if it was—she didn't care. In this hot weather no one could concentrate anyway. And she knew Mr. Burns, her sixth-grade teacher, would never punish her for missing class. Last term she had all *A*'s on her report card and an almost perfect attendance record.

Besides, she thought as the belches grew fainter and fainter, now she wouldn't have to put up with Missy's chatter on the bus, or Curtis's snotty remarks, or Doreen's airs. Maybe she would never go back. Maybe she would just live out here in the woods like Sam in *My Side of the Mountain*, a book about a boy who lived for months in a hollowed-out tree, cozy as a turtle. Crossing her arms over her chest, she gazed at the sky through lace-covered branches.

And then, just as she was beginning to feel safe again, Flora sensed that she wasn't alone. She sat forward. "Gram!" she cried, and suddenly tears were pouring down her cheeks. Unable to hold in the sobs she'd been holding back for so long, she cried and cried till no more tears would come. Finally, her breath still coming in painful gasps, she stopped to listen to a new sound in the distance—the *rrahrr . . . rrahrr . . . rrahrr* of the pickup's engine, growling to a start. Her uncle must be leaving for work, she thought. He'd been a mail carrier in Kentucky and had been assigned the same job with the Roseville Post Office. With him gone, the only ones left at home now would be Abbie and Pollyann.

The early morning air wound around Flora like a cocoon, close and silent. *Too* silent, she thought. Why had Aunt Abbie stopped calling her? Didn't she care where she was? Wasn't she worried?

Not knowing what else to do or where else to go, Flora slipped down out of the tree and headed for home.

THREE

The Riddle

WHEN Flora returned to the house, Pollyann was banging on a toy xylophone in the living room while Aunt Abbie watered Gram's African violets that filled the bay window. The two of them had the same pumpkin-colored hair, only Pollyann's formed a halo of curls around her head while Abbie pulled hers back rather carelessly in a barrette at the back of her neck. Neither of them noticed Flora standing in the doorway.

Flora gazed around the room where she and her grandmother had spent their evenings playing Scrabble, sewing, reading to each other, sipping cocoa in front of the fire. The furniture was patched and worn, but the room was alive with color: red calico pillows on the sofa; braided rugs on the floor; a fat blue jug full of cattails by the fireplace; and floor-to-ceiling bookcases crammed with books of every size and description.

When Abbie turned around and saw Flora standing there,

she didn't ask her where she had been. She just smiled and said, "I love African violets, don't you? The colors are so bright—like purple stars."

Flora stared at the floor and didn't answer.

"I'm sorry about the cup," her aunt added quietly. "Missy feels awful bad about it, too. If she hadn't been scufflin' with Curtis, it wouldn't have happened—but you know Missy. She can't seem to stop her fidgetin' and squirmin'. Seems to be part of her nature."

Still Flora said nothing.

"I kept the pieces for you. Wrapped 'em in an old bandanna. No use tryin' to glue 'em together, though—all those itty-bitty slivers."

Flora knew Abbie was waiting for her to say something, but she didn't want to cry again, so she just nodded her head.

"Would you like somethin' to eat?" Abbie asked her. "You took off so fast you never touched your pancakes."

"No thanks," Flora murmured, though her stomach was hollow as a drum. "I'll go on up to my room and do some homework."

"All right, honey. You run along."

Flora took the bandanna full of broken china that Abbie handed her and carried it upstairs to the bedroom that she now shared with Missy. No one had asked her how she felt about that. Doreen had moved all her stuff into what used to be Gram's sewing room—no more than a cubbyhole, really. She said that after sharing a room with Missy for seven years she deserved a room of her own, and her parents agreed. "Missy can sleep with Flora," they declared. The next thing Flora knew, they'd marched into her room and started pushing furniture around, and Missy's cot ended up in the corner where

15

an old washstand had been. "No one uses washstands anymore," Abbie had said. "We'll just haul this old thing up in the attic and get it out of the way."

I use it, Flora had wanted to tell her. I *look* at it. I rub my fingers over the wood sometimes because it's old and I like the way it feels—soft, like velvet.

But Flora could tell that *use* meant something different to the Quiggs, and she hadn't tried to explain.

After closing the door that she wished now had a lock, Flora opened the top drawer of her dresser. Reaching way back under her underwear, she pulled out a blue silk pouch tied with a gold cord. When she untied the cord, a small block of wood slipped into the palm of her hand. Its edges were rounded, and the wood had been polished to such a high gloss that it gleamed like satin. A tiny heart carved from a darker wood was inlaid in one corner. The block appeared to be solid, but when Flora pressed her thumb against one edge, the top slid back, revealing a hollowed-out place inside. And tucked into the hollow place was a tightly folded piece of paper.

Glancing nervously at the door, Flora settled herself against the pillows on her bed. Then, with the point of a straight pin, she lifted the paper out of the box. Unfolding it carefully, she read the words that her grandmother had written in small, shaky handwriting:

Tall, dark, handsome—
straight they stand,
many fingers
on each hand.

16

Gifts they carry,
sweet and small
in chests that swing
and sway, then fall.

Guard them well,
and love them, too—
for treasure they
will bring to you.

A month before she died, Flora's grandmother had reached under her pillow and pulled out the silk pouch which she had placed in Flora's hand. "My father carved this box for me when I was five years old," she told Flora. "I still remember him saying, 'A tiny box for a tiny girl,' as he laid it in my hand."

Flora had felt her grandmother's thoughts traveling back over the years. "Now it holds a secret—a special gift for you."

Flora had kissed the old woman's wrinkled cheek and laughed at the twinkle in her eye. "Everything in your life has a secret, Gram!" But even as she'd said it, sadness began settling around her like snow.

It hadn't taken Flora long to find the secret compartment and the hidden verses. Of course she'd wanted to know right away what the verses meant, but Gram refused to tell her. "You're a clever girl," she'd said. "When the time is right, the message will be clear."

When the time is right. That puzzled Flora as much as the verses. How would she know when the time was "right"? Would there be some kind of sign? A lightning bolt? A shape in the clouds? She wished she knew. With Gram gone, she wondered if she would ever discover the answer to the riddle.

Flora folded the paper and tucked it back in the little hollow. Then she kissed the box, slipped it into the pouch, and returned it to her dresser.

When a knock sounded at her door, Flora opened it reluctantly. Aunt Abbie's smile was apologetic. "Flora honey, I hate to interrupt you when you're workin', but I need to go down cellar and do some laundry, and it would be such a help if you could watch Pollyann for me. Last time she dumped soap powder all over the wet clothes just as I was ready to hang 'em up, and I had to wash the whole batch over again."

Pollyann darted past Flora and began pulling books off her desk and letting them drop to the floor.

Abbie grinned. "Looks like Pollyann wants you to read to her," she said. "I never seem to have time for that."

Before Flora could think of a way to worm out of it, Abbie said, "Thanks loads!" and was off down the stairs, leaving Flora alone with the dreaded Pollyann who preferred eating books to reading them.

Flora sighed. She picked up her books and piled them on a shelf where Pollyann couldn't reach them. Pollyann squinched up her face and started to howl. "Book!" she wailed. "Book! Want book!"

Flora wasn't used to babies and didn't know what to do. She wasn't about to let Pollyann chew up her math book, or any of her other books for that matter. She sat on her bed and patted the spot next to her, coaxing Polly to come the way she used to coax Guffer, Gram's old collie who had died last year. "Come on, Polly," she said. "Come on up here and I'll show you something."

Pollyann didn't budge, but her howling ebbed to a snuffle. She looked at Flora. "*Book*," she repeated, and stuck her lower lip out as far as it would go.

Flora got up and rummaged in her closet until she found a book her mother used to read to her when she was very small: *The Poky Little Puppy*. She held it out so that Pollyann could see the picture of the puppy on the cover. Pollyann sucked her lip in and grinned. "*Wead!*" she commanded, and climbed up onto the bed next to Flora.

THE MORNING seemed endless. Flora couldn't get a lick of work done. Pollyann kept getting into things and Aunt Abbie kept tromping up and downstairs, asking her one thing or another. After lunch Flora went outside to weed the flower garden, and had just come in to wash up when the back door burst open.

"Mama, Curtis stole my rocks!" screeched Missy, dumping her lunchbox on the kitchen table.

"Did not!" Curtis retorted.

"Did so! You threw them away and I'll never find 'em!"

Curtis slammed one cupboard door after another, looking for something to eat. "They weren't good rocks anyway, bird-brain. They were *gravel*."

"They were so good rocks! They *sparkled*! I was going to give them to Flora."

Hearing her name gave Flora a jolt. Her cousins' constant bickering made her nervous, even sick to her stomach, and she tried to shut it out by not listening. But Missy insisted on dragging her into things—like now, telling Curtis those rocks were for her. Why would Missy want to give her a bunch of old rocks anyway?

Aunt Abbie appeared in the doorway with Pollyann thrashing like a fish in her arms. "How many times have I told you all to come in *quietly*," she scolded them, "so you won't wake Polly from her nap? Now we'll have to put up with her bein' cranky till bedtime."

"Curtis stole my rocks," Missy tattled to her mother.

Abbie ignored her. "Doreen, put that fruit Jell-O right back in the fridge. It's for supper. And don't touch the tapioca pudding either."

"Well, for cripes sake, what *can* we eat around here?" Doreen complained.

"Here, have a banana!" Curtis tossed one at her. "It's rotten, like you."

"Ha ha, very funny," said Doreen, catching it and stuffing it down his shirt.

Missy clamped her hands on the back of a chair and started jumping up and down like a cricket. The heels of her cowboy boots clattered against the linoleum. "Look, Mama! Look, Doreen! See my shadow on the floor? See how it looks like a giraffe when I jump real high?"

Nobody looked. Missy kept jumping. "Look, now it's a monster with horns! It gets bigger and smaller and bigger again." She kicked her leg in the air and knocked a glass of milk out of Doreen's hand. The glass didn't break, but milk sloshed from one end of the kitchen to the other.

"Honestly, Missy, somebody oughta lock you up!" Doreen grabbed a dish towel and dangled it in front of her. "Now get busy and mop up that mess! We're about out of milk as it is."

Missy knelt on the floor and swished the towel through the puddles. Then suddenly she stopped and gazed up at Flora with the biggest eyes Flora had ever seen—like pools you could fall right into. "Do shadows have shadows?" she asked her solemnly.

"Ignore her," Curtis advised. "She asks dumb questions all the time. Don't answer her."

"But I want to *know*," Missy persisted.

Flora deliberated a moment, then said, "I don't think shadows have shadows, Missy."

"Why don't they?" Missy demanded.

"Because there's nothing really there, I guess. Shadows are just—*shadows*."

"See, I told you." Curtis was trying to balance an orange on his finger. "Talking to her is like talking to a chipmunk."

"If I'm a chipmunk, then you're a baboon," Missy sassed back.

Flora was getting a headache. She turned to leave, but Missy caught her around the ankle.

"I'm sorry I broke your cup, Flora."

"Missy, let go of my leg."

"I'm reallyreallyreally sorry. I'll get some superglue and stick the pieces together and make it just like it was."

"Missy, *let go of me!*" Flora shook her leg so hard that she kicked Missy's chin.

Missy let out a yelp and released Flora's leg. "I'll fix it like new!" she shouted as Flora ran for the door. "I will! I promise!"

FOUR

The Willapus-Wallapus

WITH Missy still shouting at her from the back door, Flora ran straight for the woods. Unlike the noisy, brawling house she'd just left, the woods were cool and still; and Flora slowed her pace to lose herself in the quiet beauty that surrounded her.

Then suddenly she stopped. Was that a twig that had snapped behind her? Or had she imagined it?

Her scalp prickled, and she turned around. Something red streaked from tree to tree across the path. She caught her breath, then saw it was only a cardinal chasing his mate. A squirrel skittered across a stump and disappeared. Then, except for the soft rushing of the creek, the woods were still.

Flora made her way to the bank, moving cautiously, her ears alert to every new sound. She was angry with herself for feeling scared. No one knew these woods better than she did.

If there *was* someone following her, they'd be sorry. She could lead them in circles until they were dizzy.

She had just begun to relax, convinced she'd been imagining things, when she heard something that set her heart pounding again. A voice—she was sure of it—calling, or crying, she couldn't tell which.

Quickly she ducked behind a clump of bushes and listened. The faint cry came again. "Oh, no-o-o-o!" Flora moaned, shutting her eyes tight. "It can't be! It just *can't* be!"

But it was. She'd know that squeaky little voice anywhere. How had Missy managed to follow her all the way to the creek? she wondered. What did she want? All Flora knew was that she didn't want Missy or anyone invading her territory. This was *her* woods, and no one else was welcome here. Especially not a motormouth pest who asked a hundred questions a minute and never stood still.

One way to get rid of her would be to stay hidden and wait for her to go away. The trouble was, Missy would probably get lost trying to find her way home. In fact, she was probably lost now or she wouldn't be yelling.

Blast it all, thought Flora, she supposed she would just have to go fetch her and haul her back home.

She backtracked as quickly as she could and found Missy, with her arms straight out like wings, teetering back and forth on a tippy rock in the middle of the creek. When she saw Flora, her face opened into a giant grin of relief and triumph.

"Look at me, Flora!" she cried. "I'm a tightrope walker at the circus! If I fall, I'll be swooshed down a giant waterfall, never to be seen again!"

"Honest to Pete," muttered Flora, leaping from rock to rock until she could almost reach Missy's hand. "Here, grab hold."

Missy grabbed.

"There are no giant waterfalls around here, and if you'll stop hopping around, you won't fall." Flora made no effort to mask her anger. "What are you doing out here anyway?"

"I was following you, but you went too fast. I wanted to see where you go when you disappear into the woods."

"Well, it's none of your business where I go," said Flora as she half led, half pulled Missy across the remaining rocks to the creek bank. "It's dangerous out here. You shouldn't have come alone. You could have run into a . . . a willapus-wallapus."

"A *what*?"

"A willapus-wallapus." Flora didn't know where it came from—but there it was. *Willapus-wallapus.* And now that she'd said it, it seemed just the thing to scare Missy a little—just enough to keep her from snooping around in the woods by herself.

"Willapus-wallapuses live in honey locust trees," Flora informed her as they threaded their way back through the woods toward the house. "Honey locusts have huge thorns like spears that can poke right through you as if you were butter. There's one now!" She pointed at a tree just ahead of them with clusters of wicked-looking thorns thrusting out from the bark like porcupine quills.

Missy shrieked and clutched Flora's arm. "Is the willapus-wallapus going to get us?" she whimpered.

"Not if we feed it something," Flora replied. She reached in her pocket to see what was there: two blue jay feathers, a penny, a gum wrapper, and a purple jellybean. She picked up the jellybean and tossed it to the tree. "Willapus-wallapuses can't resist sweet things," she informed Missy, "—especially jellybeans. Remember to carry some with you whenever you're in the woods because you never know when the willapus-wallapus might be lurking around, waiting to catch you."

Once they were safely past the honey locust tree, Missy relaxed her grip on Flora's hand, but only a little. "Why do trees have thorns?" she demanded.

Oh boy, here we go, Flora thought. The Question Machine. "They have thorns so they can poke little girls who talk too much."

Her curt reply silenced Missy, but only for a moment. "Ooogh! What're *those*?" she asked, pointing at a rotting log covered with spongy white bumps. "They're *creepy!*"

It was hard to believe that Missy had never seen bracket mushrooms before, but her ignorance of life in the woods made it even easier for Flora to fool her. "They're *blumps*," said Flora. "And don't ever brush against a blump because if you do, they'll start growing all over you."

"Ooooooo!" wailed Missy. "I don't like it in here! I wanna go home!" She shuddered, pulling on Flora's arm, but Flora refused to move any faster. It made her feel mean inside, telling those lies, but she couldn't stop herself. She wanted to be alone—she *had* to be alone—and she knew she never would be again if Missy was going to traipse after her all the time. Anyway, she told herself, Missy was too little to be out here alone. All kinds of things could happen to her. She could get into poison ivy, or lose her way, or fall in the creek, or . . .

Missy was silent as a shadow the rest of the way home. She didn't move with Flora's long-limbed grace, but clumped awkwardly along in her oversized cowboy boots.

"Why do you wear those clunky things?" Flora asked irritably. "Boots like that are for horseback riding, not hiking."

"They're my good-luck boots." Missy lifted her tiny chin defensively. "I got them for my birthday, and I wear them *everywhere.*"

When they finally broke out of the woods and saw Curtis bouncing a volleyball against the house, Missy couldn't help shouting, "Hey Curtis! Flora rescued me from the willapus-wallapus!"

"Too bad," Curtis called back. "She should've let it gobble you up."

Curtis could be a real snot, thought Flora, like all the other ten-year-old boys she knew. Never in her wildest nightmare did she ever imagine she'd have to live in the same house with one. Thank heaven he had allergies. The shots he got were supposed to help, but he still didn't venture much into the woods for fear he'd start to wheeze.

Missy stuck her tongue out at her brother as she marched past him to the house. Then she turned and waited for Flora who was standing uncertainly in the middle of the yard. "Aren't you coming?" she asked her.

"Nope, I'm staying here," Flora replied. "I want to be by myself, so don't follow me this time."

Missy's face fell. "Okay," she said softly. "Are you going back to the . . ."

"I don't know where I'm going," Flora snapped, "—so don't ask." Choked-down tears made her voice sound harsher than she'd intended.

She wandered over to the swing that hung from the branch of an oak tree in back of the house. Grabbing the ropes, she pushed off and leaned back, closing her eyes as the swing lifted her up, floated her down, lifted her again. All she'd wanted was to be alone in the woods this afternoon—to search for wildflowers and to sit in her tree.

As usual, Missy had spoiled everything. Even if Flora went back to the woods now, it wouldn't be the same. *She* wouldn't be the same. Her confrontation with Missy had left her with a sour feeling inside, like cider gone bad. Why was that kid so gullible, she wondered? So easy to scare?

Then, pushing her thoughts aside once more, she pumped herself higher and higher into the air. So high that for a moment nothing mattered but soaring up and up and up—as far from the earth as she could go.

FIVE

The X

UNABLE TO sleep that night, Flora lay in bed watching the moon drift like a silver boat among the stars. For a few moments she forgot she wasn't alone in her room—forgot that Gram wasn't sleeping in the big bed across the hall. Then Missy's voice jolted her back to reality.

"Flora? Do you still hate me for breaking your cup?"

"I thought you were asleep, Missy."

"I can't sleep. I keep thinking about the cup."

"Well, forget it. It was an accident. And accidents happen, that's all."

"But that cup was so old. Your grandmother drank out of it for years and years and years. Then I came along and broke it."

"Missy, it's okay. Really. Now go to sleep."

"Flora?"

Flora sighed. "Yes, Missy?"

"Mama says you and me are half-cousins, so was your grandmother partly my grandmother, too?"

Flora paused. This could be complicated. But she would try to make it as simple as possible so the two of them could get some sleep before the sun came up.

"The answer to your question is no, we have different grandmothers—at least on our mothers' side—because our mothers are only half-sisters. They had the same father but different mothers."

"How come?"

Oh boy. Flora took a deep breath. "Because after my mother, whose name was Dawn, was born, her father—that's our grandfather—divorced Gram and married your grandmother. They had a daughter named Abbie, who is your mother. That made Dawn and Abbie half-sisters."

The social worker, Miss Kimball, had explained all this to Flora after Gram died. She said the reason Gram had never mentioned the Quiggs to Flora was probably that Gram had been badly hurt when her husband divorced her and married the woman who turned out to be Abbie's mother. Miss Kimball told Flora that Gram probably didn't want to think about her ex-husband's new family. But, when she realized there was no other living relative to take care of Flora after she died, she must have decided to include them in her will—but only if they agreed to take care of Flora.

"Your mother's dead, isn't she?" Missy asked suddenly.

Flora rolled toward the wall, pulling a blanket around her shoulders. "Yes."

"Who's your father?"

"I don't have a father."

"That's not true. Everybody has a father."

"Okay, I have a father." Flora's words were sharp as the honey locust thorns in the woods. "His name is Jake. Jake the Jerk. That's all I know. My mother loved him, I guess. At least she married him. Then as soon as I was born, he took off and never came back."

"Why not?"

"How should I know?" Flora snapped. "He didn't like babies, I guess."

"Don't you ever see him—or talk to him? Doesn't he send you money or anything?"

"Nope, nope, and nope. He just vanished. That's what people do when you love them. They vanish. Just wait. You'll see."

Flora's accusing tone silenced Missy, but only for a moment. "Why are you mad at me, Flora?"

Flora groaned. "I'm not mad at you, Missy. I'm tired, that's all. And I'm not answering any more questions. So, *goodnight.*"

Flora pulled her pillow over her head and closed her eyes. But it was a long time before she slept.

AFTER SCHOOL the next day, while the others were fighting over which TV program to watch, Flora slipped off to the woods to be by herself. The air was gentle, like a soft hand caressing her face. She fished a blue stone out of the creek, then played a game with herself as she walked along, seeing how many of the wildflowers she could name.

When her maple tree finally came into view, a breeze ruffled its topmost branches so that it seemed to be waving at her. She waved back, and began to run. In a single graceful motion she scaled the trunk and swung herself up into the branches, now hung with delicate sprays of yellow-green flowers that spread like a canopy over her head.

Flora wondered what it would be like to be a tree—to sleep through the winter and grow new leaves every spring. What if people could do that? she thought. Then Gram might have replaced her worn-out heart with a new one . . . and her mother might have been able to grow new cells without cancer in them . . .

She stopped herself. It was useless, imagining things that could never happen. At least her tree would be here always. It was strong and solid. Perched up here on top of the world, Flora could see in every direction. Behind her was the yellow house where she had lived all her life—five years with her mother and grandmother, and then—after her mother died—six more years with Gram.

Flora's gaze turned from the house in the distance to the deserted farmyard below. Looking down at the clearing, Flora could just make out two faint tracks that years ago had been a road winding through the woods to the highway. Then her eyes grew heavy and she fell asleep, cradled in the arms of her tree.

By the time Flora woke, the shadows had lengthened and the air had grown cool. Quickly she scrambled down and headed for home, fearing that one—or all—of the Quiggs might come searching for her if she didn't show up in time for supper.

The fastest way through the woods led through a grove of walnut trees that grew alongside the old overgrown driveway. Flora was so intent on getting home that when she passed a tree with a bright orange X painted on its trunk, she went right on by without stopping. It was only later, in the middle of supper, that she thought about what she had seen.

"Uncle Walter," she said, tapping gently on his arm to get his attention, "why do you think someone would paint an X on a tree?"

"An X?" He frowned. "I have no idea, Flora."

"Hey, Dad," Curtis interrupted, "I need a shelf for my rock collection. Can we go to K-Mart tomorrow and get brackets and stuff?"

"And while you're at it," Doreen said scornfully to Curtis, "why don't you go to the Ugly Department and get some new parts for your face?"

"You just shut up!" Curtis shot back.

"Okay, okay, hold it down, you two." Walter waved his arms over the table like a referee separating a pair of wrestlers. He picked up the salad bowl and offered it to Flora. "More salad?" he asked her.

She shook her head and passed it on to Missy. Obviously her uncle had forgotten her question—if he'd ever really heard it at all.

SIX

Thunderstorm

AT THE first faint rumble of thunder, Flora heard Pollyann whimpering and the muffled voice of Aunt Abbie trying to comfort her.

"*I'm* not afraid of thunder," Missy announced staunchly as she peered across the room at Flora. "I *like* it. It sounds like tigers growling."

Just then a flicker of lightning swept the walls, and the growls grew louder and closer. "How 'bout you, Flora?" Missy's voice was starting to tremble. "Are you scared of thunderstorms?"

Flora didn't answer. She was remembering a long time ago when she was so terrified of storms that she would bury her head under the covers at the faintest rumble of thunder. Then one night during a furious storm, her mother had slipped silently into her room, lifted her from her bed, and carried her to the window. Safe in her mother's arms, she had watched the wind and rain lash the tree branches, and had thrilled each time the lightning lit the backyard with its bright eerie glimmer.

"I used to be afraid," she said, almost to herself, "but I'm not anymore. Storms . . . *excite* me," she whispered. "They make me feel . . . I don't know . . . *alive.*"

The next clap of thunder sounded like an avalanche of boulders crashing down a mountainside.

"*Floraaaaaaaa!*" Missy's voice was tinged with panic. "Can I come get in bed with you?"

Flora didn't like the idea of sharing her bed with a squirmer like Missy, but finally relented. "Okay, come on. But just till the storm is over."

Missy dragged her pillow and favorite blanket over to Flora's bed. For a long time they were both quiet, listening to the rain and the wind and the thunder. Then, when Flora was almost asleep, Missy turned to her and said, "Mama and Daddy think you're strange."

Flora came awake fast. "What do you mean, *strange?* What did they say?" She raised up on one elbow and peered intently at the small round face beside her.

"They were talking in the kitchen after supper," said Missy, "and I heard Mama tell Daddy that you're 'a strange one,' that's all."

"Well, why did she say that? What else did they say? *Tell* me, Missy."

Missy yawned. "Just that you go off by yourself all the time . . . and you never say anything."

"Never *say* anything? What am I supposed to say? Maybe it's just that they don't listen."

Suddenly her stomach hurt. She lay back down and tried not to think. But the more she tried, the more her head filled with memories: Gram brushing her hair before she went to sleep . . . Gram sitting with her when she had bad dreams . . . her mother rocking her during thunderstorms . . . rocking and rocking . . . *strange* . . . *doesn't talk* . . . *goes off by herself* . . . rocking, rocking . . . BOOM! . . . thunder rolling . . . rolling . . . rolling away . . .

THE NEXT thing Flora knew, it was morning. Sunlight glistened through raindrops strung like beads on branches outside the window. And there was Missy, still curled beside her, sunlit hair fluffed out on the pillow like a dandelion gone to seed.

Today was Saturday. Flora remembered Aunt Abbie saying something about shopping at the mall. Flora hoped she wouldn't have to go. She hated the mall, especially on Saturdays when everybody in the world was there.

She hadn't always hated it, though. She used to like going with Charlotte Ruggles and her mother because they always ended up at Figaro's for hot fudge sundaes. But Charlotte never asked her to go anymore. Not since she started taking baton lessons and hanging around with boy-crazy Marnie Kostakos and Angela Pratt. Charlotte had been Flora's best friend all through fourth and fifth grades, but now it was like the two of them lived on different planets.

For one painful moment, Flora wondered if Charlotte had deserted her because, like Abbie, Charlotte thought she was strange. Then she pushed the thought aside. So what if she *was* strange? There were lots worse things a person could be. Like snotty, for instance. Or stuck-up. Or mean. Besides, she could live without Charlotte Ruggles. She could live without *anybody*, especially the Quiggs.

What Flora really wanted to do today was to find her way back to that tree she'd passed yesterday with the orange *X* painted on it. How long had it been there, she wondered? And why hadn't she noticed it before?

"Sure you won't change your mind and come with us, honey?" Aunt Abbie asked again, applying a quick dash of color to her lips at the hall mirror. "It would do you good."

"No thanks," said Flora, "I'd rather stay here. I'll be fine. Really."

Uncle Walter, waiting outside with the others in the pickup, tooted the horn impatiently. Abbie flew to the kitchen for her purse, tucked Pollyann's teddy bear under one arm, then lingered in the doorway with an uneasy glance at Flora. "You're sure now?" she asked one last time.

Flora smiled. "I'm sure. You all go on now. Have a good time!"

As soon as they were gone, Flora went straight to the kitchen and snapped off the TV that had been blaring away since daybreak. Sometimes the uproar in this house made her feel like she was living in a bus station. Standing by the window, drenched in late April sunlight, she closed her eyes and let the warmth lap at her like quiet ripples off a lake.

When she opened her eyes she found herself staring at a sink full of dirty dishes. There had been so much wrangling that morning over whose turn it was to wash them that they never had got done. Without thinking what she was doing, Flora set about washing the dishes herself and setting the kitchen to rights. It made her feel good to have things in order.

Once the dishes were done, she headed straight for the

woods. The ground was still damp underfoot, and sunlight streamed through the latticework of leaves overhead, dappling the forest floor with golden freckles. "Hi guys!" she called to a tuft of buttercups poking up beside a stump. "And you too!" she called to the chickadee chittering over her head.

The woods were so lovely this morning that Flora almost forgot why she had come. But she remembered in a hurry when the X appeared before her on the walnut tree. This time she went up and examined it closely. It was about a foot high and painted in bright orange paint that seemed to glow. Phosphorescent paint? But why would someone use that on a tree—unless they wanted to find it again in the dark? And who had been in here anyway? This was private property. Whoever it was had definitely been trespassing.

Her own questions were beginning to frighten her.

Now that she'd found it again, Flora wished she'd never seen the X in the first place. Of course it was possible that it had been here a long time—months maybe—and she just hadn't noticed it. Even so, it gave her a creepy feeling knowing that someone—a stranger—had been here in the woods. *Her* woods. Maybe on this very spot.

SEVEN

Jellybeans and Dandelions

IT WAS nearly noon by the time Flora returned to the house. The silence—so welcome before—made her uneasy now, so she sat outside on the swing, wondering what to do.

If she told her aunt and uncle about the X, then right away they would want to see it. Uncle Walter would go marching out there with the whole family traipsing after him. Then he'd tell her not to go in the woods anymore, and . . .

I won't tell them, she decided. *I'll just keep watching the tree and see what happens. Maybe the X has been there for weeks—or months—and I've never noticed it before. I'm probably getting riled up over nothing. For all I know, it could be marking a property line—or an electrical cable under the ground. People put marks on trees for all kinds of reasons.* Relieved, she pumped herself higher and higher in the swing, forgetting everything but the heady climb up, the dizzy swoop down. . . .

"FLORA! Flora! We're home!"

Missy bounded to the swing like a rambunctious puppy. "I'll bet you can't guess what I've got in this sack!" she teased, holding it up so Flora could see it. "I spent my whole allowance on it."

Flora slowed the swing with her feet and jumped off.

"Rocks?" she guessed.

"Nope."

"Popcorn?"

"Unh-unh."

"A baby elephant?"

Missy giggled. "Nope."

"Okay, tell me. I give up."

Missy opened the sack and held it so Flora could look inside.

"Mmmmm . . . jellybeans," said Flora. "Can I have a red one? Red's my favorite."

"Okay," said Missy, "but just one. The rest are for the willapus-wallapus."

Flora frowned. "You spent your whole allowance on jellybeans for the willapus-wallapus?"

"Yep." Missy beamed with pleasure. "If we feed him all these jellybeans, he won't try to hurt us when we go in the woods."

"Wait a minute, Missy." Flora didn't like the way "we" and "us" were creeping into this conversation. "How and when do you plan to feed all these jellybeans to the willapus-wallapus?"

Clutching her sack with both hands, Missy bunny-hopped toward the house. "This afternoon!" she called over her shoulder. "We can go to the woods right after lunch. Mama said it's okay as long as you're with me. I already asked her."

"Oh, you did, did you?" Flora muttered under her breath. Then, louder: "Well, what if I've got other plans?"

Missy stopped hopping and turned to stare at Flora with her cornflower eyes. "Do you?"

Oh, Lord. It's hopeless, thought Flora. But she had to admire Missy's persistence. "I guess not. But we'll have to watch out for blumps. They're everywhere this time of year."

"Yaaaay! We're going to the woods!" Missy hopped and skipped all the way to the house while Flora followed slowly, kicking an old tennis ball and wondering what she'd got herself into now.

Sure enough, Flora regretted her decision the moment they entered the woods. With Missy jumping and chattering beside her, nothing felt the same. The magic was gone. Those mean feelings were sneaking around inside her again, making the whole world feel sour and out of tune.

If only Missy would stop *bouncing*! Up and down . . . up and down . . . yanking her arm practically out of its socket. It made Flora want to scream. Finally she turned and grabbed Missy's shoulders.

"You're a real pain, Missy Quigg—you know that?" She gave her a shake.

Missy's small form went limp and her eyes filled with tears. "I know," she whispered.

"So if you know, why don't you stop?"

"I don't know how."

"Well, don't talk so much for starters."

"But that's the only way I find out anything."

"You don't find out things by talking." Flora's voice softened. "You find out things by listening—and looking. Especially when you're in the woods."

"What do you mean?" Missy wiped her nose on the sleeve of her sweater.

Flora thought a minute. Then she remembered a poem that Gram had taught her. She recited it as they walked along:

> "To look at any thing,
> if you would know that thing,
> You must look at it long:
> To look at this green and say
> 'I have seen spring in these
> Woods,' will not do—you must
> Be the thing you see:
> You must be the dark snakes of
> Stems and ferny plumes of leaves,
> You must enter in
> To the small silences between
> The leaves,
> You must take your time
> And touch the very peace
> They issue from."

"That's nice," said Missy when Flora had finished. "I like the *ferny plumes* part best. It sounds . . . soft. Say the whole thing again."

Flora said the poem again.

Afterward, for maybe thirty seconds, Missy didn't say a word. Then she walked straight into a cobweb strung across the path and screamed so loud that Flora was sure the moles underground must be holding their ears.

"Oooogh! Get it off! It's sticky! It's all over my face!" She started spitting. "Ppthh! It's in my mouth!"

"Then *shut* your mouth," said Flora sharply. "It's only a cobweb. It's not going to kill you." She handed Missy a tissue to wipe her face.

After that, Missy walked behind Flora for protection.

"How much farther to the first porcupine tree, Flora?" she asked.

"Porcupine tree?" For a moment Flora was puzzled. Then she remembered. "Oh! You mean the honey locust tree . . . where the willapus-wallapus lives? There's one right over that next rise."

Before leaving home Flora had decided that she wouldn't take Missy beyond the creek. In fact, she had made Missy promise that she would never ever cross the creek by herself. That way Flora could be assured of at least *some* privacy. Besides, the tree with the X was on the other side of the water, and she didn't want Missy wandering around over there until she was sure it was safe.

"There it is!" she cried, pointing at a small tree with spikes poking out all over its trunk. "Got your jellybeans ready?"

Missy reached into her sack. "Ready!" she said.

"Then fire away!"

Missy stepped back and heaved a handful of jellybeans into the air. Most of them went straight up and rained down on their heads.

"Hm. Your throwing arm needs a little practice," observed Flora. "Here, give me some." Missy dribbled a few jellybeans from her sack into Flora's hand. When Flora threw them, they went flying like colored stars into the air. A few even hit the tree and bounced back.

With her hands on her hips, Missy grinned up at Flora. "That ought to keep the old willapus-wallapus happy for a while!" she exclaimed triumphantly.

Flora grinned back, then led the way to a big rock overlooking the creek where she often stopped on the way to her tree. She called it the listening rock because it was a perfect place to sit and listen to the creek rippling and rushing below.

"Sit down and close your eyes," she said to Missy, a hint of secrecy in her voice. "See how many different sounds you can hear."

Missy plopped down next to Flora. "Why do I have to close my eyes? I hear fine with my eyes open."

"Just try it," said Flora. "Come on, we'll do it together." She took Missy's hand and they closed their eyes.

"All I hear is water gurgling," Missy complained.

"Stay quiet and keep listening."

This time Missy kept quiet. When Flora said, "Okay, open your eyes," Missy said, "No! Wait! I'm still hearing things!"

Flora waited. Finally Missy opened her eyes.

"Did you hear that, Flora?" she asked excitedly. "Did you hear that bird singing?"

"Which bird? What did it say?"

Missy cocked her head, thinking. "It said, 'Squirt squirt *squirt*! Squeet squeet *squeet*!'"

Flora burst out laughing. "A cardinal! What else did you hear?"

Missy's eyes were wide with wonder. "I heard *lots* of things!

I heard a bee buzzing. I heard branches squeaking in the wind. And lots of birds. And an airplane. And somebody hammering on a house."

Flora laughed again. "That was a woodpecker hammering with his beak on a dead tree."

"What does he do that for?" Missy wondered.

"He's hunting for insects," said Flora, "because that's what he eats."

"I heard lots of sounds, didn't I?" said Missy proudly.

"More than I did," Flora admitted. "I missed the bee."

"Can we play again?"

Flora stood up and stretched. "Sure, Missy, but not right now. We'd better head back or your mom will worry."

Hand in hand they leaped off the rock and started down the path.

"Flora?"

"Yes, Missy?"

"I like you."

Flora felt a rush of warmth to her cheeks. "Even if I'm strange?"

"Mama said that, not me."

"Anyway, how can you like me? I'm not even nice to you."

"I like you 'cause you know things," Missy replied. "I want to know things, too," she added.

"You know lots of things, Missy."

"Not as much as you."

Flora was anxious to change the subject. "Here," she said, picking a dandelion that had gone to seed and handing it to Missy. "Blow on it three times as hard as you can. The number of seeds that are left will be the number of children you'll have."

Missy blew. Once. Twice. Three times. Then she counted the seeds, pulling them off one by one.

"*Fourteen?*" She looked at Flora, aghast.

Flora thought a moment. "I just remembered something," she said. "You have to pick your own dandelion to make it work. Try again."

Missy picked a large dandelion and blew again, three times. This time only five seeds were left.

"Good!" said Missy happily. "I'll have a family the same size as ours."

"But there are only four kids in your family."

"Not anymore," sang Missy. "With you there's *five*."

LATER, at supper, Flora thought again of Missy's remark. As usual, the uproar in the kitchen was deafening. Tonight the newscaster on TV had to compete with Pollyann's squalling and Curtis's dive-bomber noises as he rammed each of his French fries into a puddle of catsup. Flora was quickly learning how to shut out the noise by pulling all her thoughts inside. If she just stared at her plate and didn't look at anyone, she could almost imagine that the Quiggs weren't there.

"Flora honey?"

Flora's head snapped up. Abbie was leaning forward across the table, a puzzled expression on her face. "What were you thinkin' about so hard," she asked, "that you didn't even hear me talkin' to you?"

Flora shrugged, poking her chicken around with her fork.

"What I was goin' to tell you," Abbie said when Flora didn't answer, "was that when we were at the mall today I picked up a brochure about the Roseville Arboretum. It seems they offer all kinds of free summer classes about animals . . . birds . . . butterflies . . . trees, anything you might want. It'd be the perfect thing for you, Flora. You could be in the woods—which is where you want to be all the time anyway—but at this arboretum place you'd be around other kids your own age. It'd be so much better for you than goin' off in these woods by yourself all the time. Especially now, after . . ." She let her voice trail off. "Well, anyway, I signed you up for the first session."

Flora stopped eating. She sat rigidly in her chair, afraid she might throw up.

"Classes start the middle of June," Abbie rattled on, "—three weeks after school's out." She paused, reaching for Flora's hand. "You're not sayin' much, honey. Did you have other plans you didn't tell us about?"

Flora snatched her hand away almost violently. "You didn't even *ask* me!" she cried. "Those classes are for city kids who've never been in the woods before. Kids who scream if an ant crawls on them. Why don't you send Missy . . . or Doreen? All I know is, *I'm* not going!"

She ran upstairs and shut herself in her room.

After supper Abbie knocked on Flora's door and asked if she could come in. Reluctantly, Flora opened the door.

Abbie seated herself in the rocking chair by the window. "Flora, I don't want to force you into something you really don't want to do," she began, "but I wish you'd give those nature classes some thought before you say no. You're goin' to need *somethin'* to do this summer, and we can't afford to send you to camp, or even classes at the Y."

"But I don't *want* to go to camp," said Flora in surprise, "or take classes either. I always read a lot in the summer, and

Gram and I used to plant a big vegetable garden, and sometimes I swim in the neighbors' pond down the road, and" —she hesitated— "and I like to spend time in the woods. *These* woods," she added hastily.

Abbie pushed a strand of hair back over one ear. "I thought you'd be so pleased." She heaved a sigh and stood up slowly. "Promise me you'll think some more about it before you make a decision . . . okay, Flora? Maybe you could find a friend at school who'd take the classes with you." She hesitated in the doorway. "You need to do *somethin'* this summer to take your mind off . . . well, you know, to keep yourself busy."

Flora was too miserable to answer. She fell asleep early and slept hard all night. Sleep seemed to be her only escape.

EIGHT

Nice Bones

A FEW nights later, Flora took her math homework down to the kitchen to avoid Pollyann's racket upstairs. She was so engrossed in a percentage problem that she didn't look up when Doreen came in and sat down across the table from her. Neither of them spoke, but Flora could hear Doreen chomping her gum like a cow chewing its cud. Finally Doreen said, "Would you mind turning your head a little to the left, Flora?"

Flora narrowed her eyes, but didn't budge.

"Please, Flora? Just tilt your head a little so the light hits your face."

A sarcastic remark was forming on Flora's tongue when she looked up and saw what Doreen was doing. She was drawing a picture.

"I didn't know you could draw," Flora said wonderingly.

Doreen shrugged. "I'd rather be able to sing like Madonna,

but the truth is, I've got a voice like a frog." She smudged a pencil line with her finger. "Faces are what I do best."

Flora leaned across the table for a closer look. "Hey, that's *me*!" she said in amazement. "I could never do that. Not in a million years."

"I'm takin' art classes at the Y this summer," said Doreen. "It costs twenty dollars, but I've got enough saved from baby-sitting."

Doreen, the Makeup Queen, paying for her own art lessons? Would wonders never cease?

Doreen picked up her pencil. "Sit back the way you were," she told Flora. "I'm almost finished."

Knowing she was being watched made it impossible for Flora to concentrate on her math problems. She wished Doreen would hurry.

"You have nice bones, Flora," Doreen observed, interrupting her again.

Flora gave a snort of laughter. "Nice *bones*? Is that supposed to be a compliment?"

"Sure. Models all have good bone structures. You know, high cheekbones, nice jaw lines" —she made a face— "not little button chins like the Quiggs." She bent over the paper, working furiously, then put the tablet down and looked hard at Flora. "You know, even though our mothers were half-sisters, you don't look a bit like the rest of us. No one would ever guess we were related. I mean, everyone else on my mom's side of the family is blond and round-faced—but you're so thin and dark and" —she hesitated, searching for a word . . .

". . . *strange*," Flora said, helping her out.

Doreen made a quirky face as if she hadn't heard right. "*What?*"

49

"I'm thin and dark and . . . *strange*. Isn't that right?"

Doreen blew a big pink bubble till it popped, then sucked it into her mouth again. "I don't know," she answered. "You keep to yourself a lot. That doesn't necessarily mean you're strange."

"Different then," amended Flora. "I'm different from the rest of you. That's what you said."

"Well yeah, I guess so. But it's no big deal. I mean, it's *okay* to be different. Lots of people are different. Like your father," she blurted out, then caught herself. "I mean, he probably had dark hair and eyes like you, right?"

"Yeah . . . right," Flora mumbled, then hunched over her book, putting an end to further conversation.

AFTER school the next day, when Missy was out of the room, Flora took a large manila envelope down from her closet shelf and set it on the bed. In it was a jumble of photographs— some in color, some black-and-white, some new, others cracked and faded. She shuffled through the stack until she found the one she was looking for: a man and a woman standing in front of a motorcycle. The man was grinning and waving a pair of crutches in the air as if he'd won them at a carnival. Although the bandage on his head hid most of his hair, a few dark curls crept out around his forehead. The woman beside him was small and pretty, with long auburn hair pulled back with a green scarf. The way her head was thrown back, you knew she was laughing. They both looked young. Probably, Flora figured with a touch of bitterness, because they were happy.

Actually, Flora's mother was nearly forty years old when

that picture was taken, and her father barely thirty. They had met in the Roseville Hospital where Dawn worked as a nurse. Jake had been passing through town when a van struck his motorcycle. He and Dawn had fallen in love while she nursed him back to health, and as soon as he was well enough to be discharged, they were married. For almost a year they lived with Gram in the old yellow house. Flora was born; then Jake disappeared.

"I knew from the start he wasn't the settling-down kind," her mother had told her when Flora was old enough to begin asking questions. "But I loved him, and I married him. And even though he left us, I still have you."

Then, just after Flora's sixth birthday, her mother had died of leukemia. Gram had kept her and raised her as if she had been her own daughter.

Doreen was right, Flora thought as she studied the photograph. She wasn't like the Quiggs at all. Her hair and eyes were like her father's, and her body was like his, too—lean and angular. Once she had overheard Gram tell someone that he had been "dashingly handsome . . . but strange and wild." Flora wondered if that was true. Sometimes she wondered what her father was really like. But mostly she didn't think about him at all.

A FEW days later when Flora needed some colored pencils for a science project, she hesitated at Doreen's door, which was shut, as usual.

"Who is it?" shouted Doreen over the blare of rock music from her radio.

"It's me . . . Flora."

The shriek of saxophones subsided, and Doreen opened the door. "Oh!" She looked surprised. "Hi, Flora. C'mon in." She waved toward an unopened packing box by the window. "Have a seat."

Flora sat down. She couldn't help staring up at two giant-sized posters of rock stars Doreen had tacked up next to Gram's pressed flower pictures on the wall. Their dazzling smiles made her uncomfortable, and she shifted her gaze to an algebra book lying open on the unmade bed. Doreen plunked herself down beside it and started doodling x y z designs in the margins of her homework paper.

"I was wondering if you have any colored pencils I could borrow?" Flora asked her. "We have to draw a cross section of a tulip for science class, and I'm making a mess of it with my crayons."

"Sure." Doreen got up and rummaged through several boxes, then handed Flora a bundle of pencils fastened together with a rubber band. "I'm not exactly unpacked yet," she remarked ruefully. "Sometimes I don't bother. It's easier just to live out of boxes than have to pack them all up again."

"What do you mean?" asked Flora.

Doreen gave her a sullen look and rolled her eyes. "Well, this isn't exactly the first time we've moved, ya know."

"It isn't?"

Doreen shook her head. "Before Daddy started working at the post office, we moved all the time. He'd get a new job, and off we'd go. I've never been in the same school more'n two years."

Flora always wondered what it would be like to move. Not that she'd wanted to. She couldn't imagine living anywhere but here in this house, on this land. "That must be hard," she remarked, "—moving around all the time."

"Yeah." Doreen shrugged. "But ya get used to it." She slid off the bed and grabbed her hairbrush. "Besides, there's one good thing about moving."

"What's that?" Flora watched in fascination as Doreen bent over and brushed her hair, attacking it with furious strokes as if she were chasing out a swarm of bees.

"Well, whenever you move, you can transform yourself into somebody new," she declared, swooping back up to a standing position and patting her frizzed-out hair in front of the mirror. "I mean, if you don't like who you are, you can change into somebody else. You can look different—act different—and kids in the new place will have no idea what you were like before."

Flora considered this idea. It had interesting possibilities, all right. "Is it really that easy?"

Doreen tossed her brush on the dresser and popped her gum while she thought about it. "No, I s'pose not," she said at last. "But pretending to be somebody else is fun for a while. It's like being in a play." She paused to pick some fuzzballs off her sweat shirt. "It can get to be a drag, though," she added. "At my last school I wanted to be on the pompon squad, so I started hanging out with that crowd and dressing like them and acting like them and everything. They liked me and taught me the pompon routines, and we had a lot of fun. But then I went to one of their parties and found out they were into alcohol in a big way. That's not my scene, so when pompon tryouts came along I didn't go. After that they dropped me like a rotten apple." She chuckled to herself. "When Dad told us we were moving to Indiana, he thought I'd throw a fit because it was so near the end of school. When I told him I was *glad* we were moving, he didn't believe me. He thought I was kidding."

Flora wondered if Doreen had decided to be her real self or a pretend-self at Roseville High School, but she didn't ask. She could see now that getting to know the real Doreen might take a long time. It might even be worth the effort.

STEADY rain plus a heavy load of homework kept Flora from exploring the woods again for over a week. The first Saturday in May, however, dawned warm and sunny—a cloudless blue-sky day, fat with apple-blossom sweetness. Flora made up her mind the moment she woke that she would spend the entire day in the woods. A whole new array of wildflowers would be blooming, and there was something else—something that had been gnawing at her all week like a bothersome itch in her mind. The X. Was it still there? She wanted to find out.

But escaping from the house wasn't as easy as she'd hoped. Uncle Walter was working, Doreen had cheerleading practice, Abbie was shoe-shopping with Curtis and Missy, and that left Flora to baby-sit Pollyann. The morning went quickly, however, and the afternoon still beckoned like a lovely package waiting to be opened.

After lunch Flora slid the heartwood box out of its pouch into the pocket of her jeans. She liked having it close to her —liked the satiny feel of the wood against her fingers. Then, looping a pair of binoculars around her neck, she sneaked quietly down the stairs to the back door. Her concentration was so deep, however, that she almost collided with Aunt Abbie coming up from the basement.

"Going for a hike?" Abbie asked her, eyeing the binoculars.

"Uh, sort of," Flora hedged. *Please don't stop me*, she begged her aunt silently. *I need to be alone.*

"Well, before you go," Abbie said, "there's something we need to talk about. C'mon, let's sit down a minute."

Reluctantly, Flora followed her aunt to the living room and perched stiffly on the edge of the sofa. She wondered if Abbie was going to go into that arboretum stuff again. If so, she thought, it wouldn't do any good. She hadn't changed her mind about those classes.

Abbie chewed her lip and jiggled her foot as if she didn't know quite how to begin. Finally she said, "Walter an' me . . . well, we've been worried about you, Flora, spendin' so much time alone in the woods."

"But I *like* being alone." Flora set her chin defiantly. "And you needn't worry about me. I can find my way around in those woods with my eyes closed!"

"I know you can, honey, but that's not the point. The point is, the world is changin', and not always for the better. Places that used to be safe . . . well, they're not always safe anymore." She paused and took Flora's hands in hers. "From now on we want you to promise to take somebody with you when you go to the woods. Okay?"

"Like who?" Flora asked, refusing to look at her.

"Ohhhh . . . like one of *us*," Abbie replied, a little too cheerfully. "Or a friend from school."

Flora was too shocked to speak. Never walk in the woods without someone else tagging along? Never sit alone in her tree? It was cruel—and unfair! They might just as well lock her in a cage and throw away the key!

"*I'll* go with you, Flora!" Missy, who had been listening at the door, skipped into the room and threw her arms around Flora's neck. "Please take me with you . . . *please*? We could go to that rock again and play the listening game! We could talk to the birds and watch the spiders cobbing their webs!"

Abbie laughed, and without even consulting Flora, gave Missy permission to accompany her.

"You're sending Missy along to *protect* me?" Flora couldn't believe it.

"Well, not exactly *protect*," Abbie replied evasively, "but two is safer than one, and there's no one else to go with you right now." The phone rang and she jumped up to answer it.

How could this be happening to her? thought Flora as her aunt disappeared into the kitchen. It wasn't fair! All week she had been waiting for this chance to be in the woods by herself. Now Abbie and Missy had ruined it. Worse yet, if Abbie had her way, Flora knew she would never be allowed in the woods alone again.

Turning her back on Missy, she stalked to the door—and once outside, broke into a run.

"Wait up!" Missy clumped down the steps in her cowboy boots and ran stumbling after her. "You can't go to the woods without *me*! Mama said so!"

NINE

The Vanishing Tree

WHEN SHE heard Missy calling her, Flora slowed to a jog but didn't look back. Eventually Missy caught up with her and yanked on the back pocket of her jeans to make her slow down even more.

"Why'd you run off like that?" Missy demanded. "Didn't you hear Mama say I was s'posed to come with you?"

"I heard." Flora swatted Missy's hand away. "Stop hanging on me."

Missy grew silent and worked hard to keep up with Flora's long strides. Suddenly she stopped short and slapped her neck. "Ooo, I got mosquito blood all over me!" she howled, holding up her smeared fingers.

Flora shot a glance at Missy's hand, then looked away. "That's not mosquito blood—it's yours," she observed coldly. "He sucked that blood right out of you. You should've known better than to come to the woods with your arms all bare like that. The mosquitoes are going to eat you alive."

Flora knew she was being horrible to Missy, but couldn't help herself. She'd been feeling so full of hope today—so sure things would be better if only she could sit in her tree and think for a while. But now that hope was gone, and the unfairness of it all made her feel like lashing out at somebody . . . *anybody.*

"What do mosquitoes eat when there aren't any people around?" Missy wanted to know.

"How should I know?" Flora growled. "Willapus-wallapus blood, I suppose."

Missy grew silent. "You don't want me to ask any more questions, do you?" she said.

Even without looking, Flora knew Missy's lip was sticking out in a giant pout. She tried hard to think of something that would keep her happy and quiet at the same time. Reaching into her pocket, she hesitated a moment as her fingers curled around the heartwood box. Then quickly—before she changed her mind—she pulled it out and placed it in Missy's hand. "Here's something for you to look at," she said. "Gram gave it to me a few days before she died. Her father made it for her when she was a little girl, and it has a secret door that slides open—see?"

Missy slid the top back and forth with her thumb. "What's that paper inside?" she wanted to know.

Flora sighed. She should have known the box would only bring on more questions. "A riddle," she answered.

"Oh, I love riddles!" Missy exclaimed. "Will you read it to me?"

"I don't have to read it. I know it by heart."

Missy waited expectantly. "Well?"

"Oh, okay." Keeping Missy quiet was impossible: she could see that now. She might as well recite the riddle and be done with it.

" 'Tall, dark, handsome—straight they stand, many fingers on each hand," she began in a disinterested monotone. "Gifts they carry, sweet and small, in chests that swing and sway, then fall. Guard them well, and love them, too, for treasure they will bring to you.' "

"Treasure! Wow!" breathed Missy. "What is it, do you think?"

"I don't know," Flora admitted. "Gram told me I'd guess the answer when the time was right."

Missy rubbed the smooth wood against her cheek. "I think 'tall, dark, handsome' means a lot of handsome princes will bring you chests full of gold."

"Fat chance of *that*," mumbled Flora. "Anyway, why would the chests 'swing and sway' like it says in the riddle?" In spite of her anger, she was curious to know where Missy's imagination might lead.

"I know!" Missy replied eagerly. "The chests swing and sway because the princes are on a ship. There's a big storm and the princes can't keep their balance. They fall down and drop the chests—and gold spills out!"

Just then a cheerful bird interrupted them with its high-pitched "*Sweet-sweet! Chew-chew!*," and Flora grabbed her binoculars to search for the singer. "Hear that song, Missy? That's an indigo bunting. A pair of them nested in that same tree last year. Want to look?"

Missy reached for the binoculars. "Why is everything so tiny?" she wondered.

"No, no," said Flora, "you're looking through the wrong end." She turned the binoculars around. "Now do you see him? He's blue. As blue as a sapphire."

"All I see is leaves."

"Uh-oh, too late. There he goes! We'll look for him on our way back."

She led Missy to the creek bank, but just as they were starting to cross, Missy stopped to fish something out of the water. "What's this?" she asked, holding up what looked like a small gray rock about an inch long. What made it unusual was its acorn shape—rounded at one end, pointed at the other. Flora had seen lots of them in her explorations of the creek bed.

"That's a willapus-wallapus toe," she informed Missy. "They drop off in the winter and grow back in the spring."

Missy screamed and dropped the "toe" back in the water. "Oogh! Oogh! I touched a dead toe!" She rocked back and forth, clutching herself and shivering.

How could Missy really believe such a dumb story? Flora shook her head, amazed at her own persuasive powers.

The willapus-wallapus toe was quickly forgotten when they reached the other side of the creek. Now all Flora could think about was finding the *X*. She started walking faster.

"Where are we going?" Missy asked, struggling to keep up with Flora's long strides.

"To the walnut grove. There's something there I have to see."

"What is it?"

"Nothing much. Just a mark on a tree."

"Sounds boring. Couldn't we stay at the creek and hunt for stones?"

Flora didn't answer. Her feet were moving faster and faster

over the thick, matted undergrowth. When the first walnut tree came into view, she grabbed Missy's hand and started to run. Her heart was pounding with a strange mixture of fear and excitement as her eyes darted from one tree to another. Where was the *X*? Why couldn't she find it?

"Stop pulling my arm!" Missy shouted. "You're hurting me!"

Flora let go of Missy's hand and kept running, zigzagging back and forth from one tree to another. It *had* to be here. She couldn't have imagined it. It was big and orange and painted on a tree right about . . .

Ouch! Something hard and sharp-edged rammed into Flora's leg. The next thing she knew, she was sprawled on the ground, her face buried in leaves. Lifting her head, she found herself staring at a stump about a foot high. Not an old rotten stump either. This stump had been freshly cut—*sawed*, in fact, and so recently that a sprinkling of sawdust still coated the ground.

Dazed by her fall, Flora could do nothing but stare and stare at the severed stump. Who could have chopped down a tree in here? This was private property. There were NO TRESPASSING signs all over the place. It made no sense. No sense at all.

She stood up and looked around. Tire tracks! Big ones! Someone must have driven a truck up the old driveway and hauled the tree back out to the road. But why come so far? And why *this* tree?

Suddenly a terrible possibility flashed through Flora's mind. "My tree!" she shrieked, almost falling backward in her haste to turn around.

"Flora! What's the matter?"

As Flora started up the hill, Missy stumbled after her. Flora whirled around and fixed her with a withering glare. "Stop right there and don't move!" she commanded. "I'm going up this hill—and I'm going *alone*."

"No-o-o-o!" wailed Missy, still stumbling through the underbrush. "Don't leave me, Flora—I'm afraid! I forgot to bring jellybeans for the willapus-wallapus and he'll *get* me!"

Too frightened herself to comfort Missy, Flora plunged on, climbing and climbing, refusing to look back. Finally a loud crackle forced her to glance over her shoulder. And there was Missy, struggling through a bramble patch and whimpering like a puppy.

"Missy Quigg, if you take another step—" Flora threatened her, "I'll . . . I'll feed you to the willapus-wallapus myself!" Then, working hard to control her own fear, she said very slowly, "Turn around now and sit on that stump till I get back. I'll only be gone a few minutes, I promise."

As soon as Missy turned around, Flora scrambled the rest of the way up the hill. Each breath was a painful gasp. What if her tree wasn't there? What if it, too, had been chopped down, with nothing left but a jagged stump?

Pausing at the crest of the hill, she clamped her hands over her eyes. Blood pounded in her ears. Hardly daring to breathe, she spread her fingers one by one and slowly opened her eyes.

The rush of relief she felt when she saw her tree standing whole and alive was so overwhelming that Flora's legs almost folded like jackknives beneath her. She raced across the clearing and threw her arms around the trunk. The bark felt rough and warm against her cheek. Trembling with relief, she leaned against her tree and closed her eyes.

TEN

Empty Pockets

SOMEONE was watching her. She knew it, even with her eyes closed.

Flora held very still. She opened her eyes and looked around. Nothing moved. Then, on the other side of the clearing, leaves rustled.

"Who's there?" she shouted.

A small figure emerged from the shrubbery, pink-faced and panting.

"Don't be mad, Flora! Please don't!"

Encumbered by her cowboy boots, Missy tottered across the clearing like a frightened calf. She snatched Flora's hand and swung it back and forth as she poured out excuses.

"I was scared to stay alone 'cuz there were noises and shadows and the willapus-wallapus was coming after me, I know he was, so I had to come find you!"

"Missy, I don't really think . . ."

But Missy's attention had shifted suddenly. She dropped Flora's hand and bent sideways to peer around her. "Why were you hugging that tree?" she asked.

Realizing now that Missy had been spying on her the whole time, Flora's lips tightened into a hard line. *I can't do anything alone now*, she thought. *Not walk in the woods—not sit in my tree—not anything.*

"Why aren't you answering me?" Missy demanded.

"Because you're a scaredy-cat and a snoop, and I'm mad at you. We're going home now."

Flora led Missy back the way they'd come, down the hill and along the edge of the walnut grove. But just as they were approaching the spot where Flora had tripped on the stump, she saw something that stopped her dead in her tracks. Another *X*! It was bright orange, just like the one on the tree that had been chopped down!

What did it mean? What was going on? Flora hurried Missy past the tree before she had time to see the *X* and start asking more questions.

There had to be a simple explanation. This time Flora made up her mind to tell Walter and Abbie about the *X* as soon as she got home. Maybe they already knew something about it. Maybe she was getting herself all worked up over nothing.

"WHERE's Mama?" Missy asked Curtis, who was busy dismantling an alarm clock on the kitchen table when they walked in.

"Grocery shopping with Dad," he mumbled, not looking up. "And whatever you do, don't make noise," he warned them. "Pollyann's sleeping. If she wakes up I have to baby-sit."

Flora washed the cut on her leg and covered it with a Band-Aid from a box on the windowsill. "Have your folks been gone long?" she asked Curtis. "Did they say when they'd be back?"

"Naw, they didn't say," he replied, "but it'll be a while because they just left."

Flora poured two glasses of lemonade and handed one to Missy. Too jumpy to sit down, she began pacing around the kitchen like a fox in a cage. She reached deep into one jeans pocket and found nothing. Then she reached in the other pocket, but all she found were cookie crumbs and a penny.

Suddenly she realized what it was she was looking for. The box! Where was it? She felt around in each of her back pockets. Empty.

She turned to Missy who was dabbling her fingers in the puddle around her lemonade glass. "Missy, where's that little wooden box with the heart on it that I was showing you today? Do you still have it?"

Missy checked her pockets. "Nope. I gave it back to you. At least I think I did."

"Well, I don't have it, and I don't remember you giving it back."

"Well, I did," Missy insisted. "I mean, I must've because I don't have it either."

Flora sat down across from her and looked at her hard. "Missy, *think*. What did you do with the box after I gave it to you? After I told you the riddle?"

"I don't know. I can't remember."

"Well, try, Missy . . . *please*! Close your eyes and *think*!"

Flora couldn't control her rising panic. The box couldn't be lost. It just couldn't! Everything she loved was slipping through her fingers. "If you don't find that box, Missy, I'll never take you to the woods again!" she threatened. "Never!"

Missy looked frightened. Her chin trembled. "Don't be mad at me, Flora!" she pleaded. "I'll find the box! I will! I promise!" Pushing her lemonade aside, she ran out of the kitchen.

Flora listened to Missy's footsteps pattering up the stairs. A part of her wanted to follow and tell her it was all right, that losing the box wasn't the end of the world. But another part of her held back—a part that wanted to punish Missy for her carelessness. First the china cup smashed to bits, and now her precious box. It was too much to forgive.

For a moment Flora thought of returning to the woods to search every inch of the path that she and Missy had followed. But when she remembered how Missy was always abandoning the path to chase butterflies or squirrels, she realized how useless such a search would be. The box could have fallen anywhere—even in the creek.

Desperate to escape the feelings seething inside her, Flora wandered into the living room and pulled a book off the shelf—*The Cherry Orchard*, a play by the Russian author Chekhov, a favorite of Gram's. She opened the book and tried to read, but the words danced like gnats in front of her eyes. Anger boiled inside her and she couldn't concentrate. Anger at Missy for losing the box. Anger at her aunt and uncle for not letting her be alone in the woods. Anger at her mother and grandmother for dying and leaving her to the Quiggs.

An hour went by, and Flora calmed down enough to be drawn into the play she was reading. The characters seemed to be talking to each other, but actually, she discovered, they were talking to themselves. They all had troubles, but no one listened to anyone else. Eventually they just drifted apart and nothing got better. It was a depressing story and Flora put the book back on the shelf. She looked at the clock on the mantel. Five-thirty! Aunt Abbie and Uncle Walter had been gone nearly two hours. Curtis had taken Polly outside to play in the sandbox. And Doreen must have come in without Flora knowing it because her radio was blaring away upstairs.

As soon as the pickup pulled into the driveway, Flora ran outside.

"Sorry we're so late," said Walter, handing her a sack of potatoes, "but the grocery was crowded—and then we stopped on the way home to pick up some flowers for the garden."

Flora stared at the flats of pansies and marigolds and snapdragons in the back of the truck. It was the pansies that brought a lump to her throat. Pansies were Gram's favorite flower, and every spring she had planted bright clusters of them on either side of the front porch.

"Did you and Missy have a good time on your hike?" Abbie asked her on their way in.

Flora tried to clear her mind as she held the door with her free hand. "Yes, but there's something I want to ask you about. Something I saw in the woods today."

"Oh?" Walter sounded interested. He plunked two sacks of groceries on the kitchen table. "What was it, Flora?"

"I saw an X painted on a tree. It's orange—about this high"—she showed him with her hands—"and I think the paint is phosphorescent because it glows."

Walter looked puzzled. "An X that glows? Where did you see it? On our property?"

Flora nodded. "It's on the other side of the creek in the

walnut grove. I saw another tree with an X on it last week, but today when I looked for it the whole tree was gone. Somebody chopped it down."

Walter's hand froze in the air halfway to the cupboard. *"Chopped it down?"* He set down the oatmeal box he was holding. "What kind of tree was it, Flora? Do you know?"

"It was a black walnut," she replied. "I know because Gram told me that she and my grandfather planted that grove about sixty years ago, the year they were married."

"Why in the world would somebody take a tree out of our woods?" Abbie demanded angrily. "You don't s'pose kids are buildin' campfires back there, do you?"

Flora shook her head. "Kids couldn't cut down a big tree like that," she said. "Besides, I didn't see any charred logs or anything. Just a stump and a lot of branches scattered around."

Abbie finished putting the eggs away in the refrigerator. "Well, unless somebody's fixin' to build a log cabin back there, I can't see any reason for cuttin' down a tree," she commented.

"Unless . . ." Walter rubbed his jaw thoughtfully, "—unless we've got ourselves some tree rustlers sneakin' around in the woods!"

ELEVEN

Missy Is Missing

"TREE rustlers? You mean *thieves?*" Flora wasn't sure she had heard right. "Why would somebody want to steal trees?"

Walter poured himself a cup of coffee and stirred it so long that Flora thought he'd forgotten her question. He was a large man with leathery skin and piercing blue eyes. Unlike the rest of the Quiggs, he didn't talk much. But the slow, distracted way he was rubbing his jaw told her he was thinking hard about something.

"Some people I delivered mail to back in Kentucky," he said at last, "told me about havin' a couple of their trees—and I'd swear they were black walnuts—stolen off their back lot once. Said they were worth a lot of money—thousands of dollars."

Thousands of dollars! For one tree? Flora's head reeled. "You mean the X's on those trees could be markers telling somebody which trees to chop down?"

Walter set his coffee cup down and picked up the phone

book. "You know, I think this is serious enough that we oughta contact the sheriff." He dialed the number.

Flora listened as he told the sheriff what she'd seen in the woods. After he hung up, he and Flora went out on the porch while Abbie started supper. A few minutes later a car swung into the driveway and two people climbed out, a man and a woman.

"I'm Sheriff Kenning," said the tall sunburned man, extending his hand toward Walter, "and this is my deputy, Karen Alt."

Flora was surprised to see a young woman dressed in the same tan uniform as the sheriff, with a gun tucked in a holster at her waist. She admired the confident way the deputy carried herself, and the way she knew exactly what questions to ask.

Curtis had heard the sheriff's car drive in and came tearing out of the house to find out what was going on, while Doreen watched the goings-on from an upstairs window.

Suddenly Abbie appeared at the front door, her face clearly troubled. "Has anyone seen Missy?" she called to the group gathered outside. "I looked everywhere and can't find her!"

"She's not in her room?" asked Flora.

Abbie shook her head. "Not in her room, and not with Pollyann. Doreen says she hasn't seen her since she got home an hour ago."

Flora tried to remember the last time she'd seen Missy. So much had been happening it was hard to think. They'd been in the kitchen drinking lemonade after their walk . . . then Flora had asked her about the box, and . . . Oh, yes, *now* she remembered!

"The last time I saw her, she was running out of the kitchen and up the stairs."

"When was that?" Abbie wanted to know.

"Just after you and Uncle Walter left for the store, I think."

Abbie's face grew even more alarmed. "That long ago? That's over two hours. Where could she have gone?"

Something began to gnaw at Flora that she didn't want to think about—something Missy had said before she ran up-stairs. Something about the box.

"You figure she might've wandered into the woods?" the sheriff suggested. He glanced at Abbie, then Walter. "We'd be glad to keep an eye out for her while we're out there. How old is she? What was she wearing?"

Walter shook his head, smiling a little. "She's not out there," he assured them. "Missy's a little bitty thing, scared of her own shadow. She'd never go in the woods alone." He turned to Abbie. "Have you looked in all the closets? Under the beds? Knowin' her tricks, she's probably just hidin' from you. Or maybe she fell asleep somewhere."

Abbie didn't appear convinced. "I'd feel a whole lot better if I knew where she was before you all took off for the woods."

Now Flora remembered what it was that Missy had said when she ran out of the kitchen: "Don't be mad at me, Flora! I'll find the box! I promise!"

Flora dashed into the house and up the stairs to their bed-room. When she opened the bottom drawer of Missy's dresser, her heart sank. Just as she'd feared—the jellybean sack was gone. Galloping back down the stairs, she nearly collided with her aunt and uncle in the front hall. Half out of breath, she tried to explain to them what she thought might have happened.

"Missy thought I was mad at her because she lost the box that Gram gave me, and she promised over and over that she'd find it. She must have taken her jellybeans with her so the

71

willapus-wallapus wouldn't come after her, and then she went back to the woods to look for the box, and . . ."

"Whoaaa!" Uncle Walter put up his hand like a police officer blocking traffic. "Let's start over—from the beginning. Now what's all this about jellybeans and a walrus?"

Flora repeated the story as quickly as she could, leaving out the willapus-wallapus this time. By the time she finished, her aunt and uncle were beginning to believe it was possible that Missy might have returned to the woods.

"I've noticed how Missy worships you," Abbie said to Flora. "She'd do anything for you. I remember how she felt when she broke that cup, and now—if she's lost somethin' else of your grandmother's—well, she must know how terrible you'd feel."

Terrible is right. Abbie had no idea how terrible, thought Flora, but not because of a missing box. Suddenly all the mean things she'd said to Missy that afternoon came rushing back at her. If only she'd been less harsh with her . . . hadn't made her feel so guilty. The tree rustlers could be sneaking around in the woods right now, waiting for a chance to cut down more trees. If Missy had gone out there and lost her way, all because of *her*. . . . !

Flora's head filled with a strange roaring and she grabbed the banister, afraid she would faint.

"Flora?" said Abbie. "Are you all right?"

Flora closed her eyes, then opened them slowly. The roaring was gone. "I'm fine," she said. "We'd better get going."

It was decided that Sheriff Kenning, Deputy Alt, Walter, and Flora would head straight for the walnut grove. Abbie and Curtis agreed to search the yard while Doreen stayed in the house with Pollyann.

72

It took only a few minutes for Flora to lead the others to the listening rock. "This is where we were sitting today when I showed Missy the box," she told them. "If Missy came back to the woods to look for it, this is where she would've come first."

"There's no sign of her here," said Karen after searching the area. "Let's fan out separately and see if we have better luck."

WHEN twenty minutes of searching and calling brought no response, they followed the same path Flora and Missy had taken to the walnut grove. Flora showed the others the stump and the tire tracks. Then, while the others were examining the tracks, Flora found something else—something she could hardly believe she was seeing. There, half hidden among the leaves near the stump, was the little heartwood box! She picked it up . . . turned it over in her hands . . . tried to think how in the world it could have gotten here.

When she finally remembered, she drew in a sharp breath. Missy *had* returned the box to her—back at the listening rock—just as she'd said! Flora recalled now how she had reached for it just as the indigo bunting started to sing. Without even thinking, she must have dropped the box into her shirt pocket as she was grabbing for the binoculars. Then later, when she fell, it had slipped out!

So Missy *hadn't* lost the box. *She* had! And now Missy was lost because Flora had blamed her for something she didn't do.

Flora stared at the tiny box in the palm of her hand, and suddenly its weight was almost more than she could bear.

When she turned around again, the sheriff was saying to Walter, "People who steal trees take only the parts they can sell. Usually they saw the trunk into eight- or ten-foot sections right on the spot, with silencers on the saws to muffle the sound. Then they load the logs onto a truck and sell them as quick as they can to some unsuspecting lumber company." He tipped his head back, scanning the grove. "These trees are fantastic. Just the right size. They'd be worth a tidy sum, that's for sure."

But Flora could see that her uncle wasn't listening. Like her, he was far more concerned about Missy than he was about a stolen tree. Already the shadows in the woods were deepening. If they didn't find Missy soon, the woods would be dark. The melancholy "*Tu-whooo!*" of an owl sounded a distant warning through the trees. "Find her soon!" it seemed to say. "Find her s-o-o-o-o-n!"

TWELVE

A Long Night

DEPUTY ALT headed back to the house to see if Missy had turned up—and if not, to radio the department, requesting more searchers. After she'd gone, the sheriff asked Flora to draw a map of the woods on his notepad. He divided it into three sections and assigned a section to each of them.

"Flora, you go back the way we came," he told her, "and search between the creek and the house. Move quickly but don't run, or you might miss something that could lead us to your sister."

"Missy's not my . . ." But Flora decided it wasn't worth taking time to explain.

"If you find anything," the sheriff added, "or if you need us, just give three blasts on this whistle and we'll come running."

The whistle was on a long string that Flora slipped over her head. She looked up when Uncle Walter touched her shoulder.

"Blow good an' hard if you see anything," he said, and she could feel the misery behind his eyes. "Anything at all."

Flora could walk almost as fast as she could run, and it didn't take her long to return to the listening rock. Forcing herself to stand still, she took a deep breath and closed her eyes the way Gram used to do whenever she had misplaced something, like her car keys or glasses. "I just calm my mind and try to picture where I was when it disappeared," she would say.

This was different, of course, but Flora thought it might help her guess where Missy had gone if she could think back to the last time she had seen her. The kitchen. That was the last place they had been together. In her mind she pictured the two of them there after their walk—heard herself repeating the angry words she wished now she'd never spoken: *If you don't find that box, Missy, I'll never take you to the woods again! Never!*"

If only she could take back what she'd said! If only . . . But, of course, she couldn't. It was too late. All she could do now was try to imagine how Missy must have felt and what she would have done. Flora wanted to believe as Uncle Walter did that Missy would be too frightened to go into the woods alone. But Walter didn't know about the jellybeans. He didn't know that Missy believed they would keep her safe because Flora had told her so.

That was it! thought Flora with a jolt. If Missy had taken the jellybeans with her, the first thing she would do would be to sprinkle them around the "porcupine trees" to keep her safe in case the willapus-wallapus was lurking around. The first tree wasn't far, but to reach it Flora had to veer off the path and clamber up a small embankment. Sure enough, when she got there, she found jellybeans strewn all around the base of

76

the tree. But where was Missy? Where would she have gone from here?

Flora decided to walk in a circle around the tree, widening the circle about thirty feet each time she went around. Every few steps, she shouted Missy's name. Halfway through the fourth circle, she heard something. It could have been a bird or the soft creaking of a branch in the wind. But to Flora the sound of her own name was unmistakable, and she broke into a run. Crashing through saplings and shrubbery like a bear on a rampage, she shouted, "Missy, it's Flora! I'm here! I'm coming!"

FLORA found Missy curled like a comma with her back against a moss-covered log. Her face was puffy from weeping, and seeing Flora made her cry even harder. "I fell," she sobbed, "and hurt my arm. My leg hurts, too, and when I tried to walk I kept falling down." She stretched one arm up to Flora.

Flora knelt down and gently brushed Missy's hair off her forehead. "It's okay, you're not lost anymore." Then she pulled back, frowning a little. "Why did you go off like that without telling anyone where you were going?"

"I wanted to find the box so you wouldn't be mad at me," Missy mumbled. The pain in her eyes was almost more than Flora could bear. "I looked and looked, but I couldn't find it."

Flora touched Missy's shoulder. "You didn't lose the box, Missy . . . I did. It fell out of my pocket when I tripped over that stump. I found it buried in the leaves a few minutes ago." She reached in her pocket and showed Missy the box.

Missy stared at it in wonder. "I didn't lose it?"

Flora shook her head. "Nope, you gave it back to me just

like you said." She put it away and turned her attention to Missy's injuries. Her left arm was oddly twisted at the elbow, and an ugly plum-sized bump had formed on her ankle. Missy tried to raise herself, but Flora stopped her. "Don't try to get up, Missy. Wait here a little longer till I get some help. The sheriff gave me this whistle to blow if I needed him." She put it to her lips and gave three sharp blasts. Then she untied her sweater from around her waist and tucked it under Missy's head. "I'm going out on the path to blow it again. Will you be okay?"

Missy nodded. "I'm not scared anymore, but my arm hurts awful bad. You won't be gone long, will you?"

Flora grazed the tip of Missy's nose with her knuckles. "I'll be back in the flash of a grigglebug's tail!"

WALTER helped Sheriff Kenning carry Missy to the house on a portable stretcher just as night was enfolding the woods in thick summer darkness. Flora walked beside her, holding her hand and telling her the story of a little willapus-wallapus who ran away to look for a jellybean tree and got lost for three days in the Pea Soup Forest.

"Like me?" Missy asked.

Flora squeezed her hand. "Like you," she said.

"ARE YOU coming with me to the hospital?" Missy asked Flora when Walter lifted her into the pickup and settled her on Abbie's lap.

"No, but I'll be waiting for you when you come back." Flora tucked the heartwood box into Missy's hand. "It's for luck," she told her. "Hold it tight. And whenever you feel scared, rub your finger over the heart."

Missy clutched the box against her chest. "What if I lose it?" she asked anxiously.

"Don't worry," Flora assured her. "It wouldn't matter."

And she meant it.

IT WAS nearly midnight when the pickup rattled into the driveway again.

"I didn't even cry!" Missy announced proudly as Flora and Doreen and Curtis crowded around her in the kitchen to admire the impressive plaster cast on her arm.

"Geez, now I s'pose I'll be stuck doin' the dishes every night," grumbled Curtis.

"Don't feel so sorry for yourself," Missy retorted. "At least *you* can go *swimming*. The doctor said I can't go swimming for six weeks. Not until he takes the cast off."

"What about your leg?" Flora asked. "I see it's all bandaged up."

Missy yawned. "I tore a liger . . . ligle . . ."

". . . ligament," Abbie finished for her. "And now it's off to bed for all of us," she said, "or we'll fall asleep standin' up." She put an arm around Flora's shoulders and gave her a squeeze. "We haven't even had time to thank you, Flora, for what you did. If it weren't for you, Missy might still be lost out there in the woods."

Flora's throat constricted painfully. "If it weren't for me, Missy would never have . . ." She couldn't finish.

Abbie gazed at her wearily, not comprehending. "Well, whatever happened, it's over now." She cupped Flora's face

79

in her hands and kissed her lightly on the forehead. Then to all of them, "Off to bed with you now. It's been a long day."

THE NEXT morning Deputy Alt stopped by the house while the Quiggs were eating a late Sunday breakfast. When Abbie invited her to join them for scrambled eggs, Flora quickly moved over to make room for her at the table.

"I'm really glad you stopped by," said Walter. "We've been waitin' to hear what happened out there last night. Did you catch those thievin' tree-choppers?"

The deputy helped herself to some of Abbie's fluffy scrambled eggs and sausage. "Well, we staked out the area around that tree with the X," she told them, "and sure enough, around three o'clock this morning a flatbed truck loaded with logging equipment pulled into the grove. Two men jumped off the truck carrying the meanest looking chain saw I've ever seen in my life. We moved in on 'em so fast they must've thought they'd been jumped by a woods monster."

"Or a willapus-wallapus," giggled Missy.

"What happened," Karen continued, "is that a crew from a lumber company had been clearing trees off the land next to yours a few weeks ago. It seems a couple of guys on the crew spotted your walnut grove and decided to make some fast money on their own. I'm glad we caught 'em before they did any more damage to your beautiful grove back there."

Before the deputy finished her breakfast, another young woman appeared at the door who said she was from the *Roseville Gazette*. Walter pulled up another chair and Abbie poured more coffee. The reporter listened to all of their stories about what had happened, but she was particularly interested in Flora's account because, as the article in the next morning's paper stated: "Eleven-year-old Flora Haywood was the one who first discovered the X's, and it was her quick thinking that eventually led to the capture of the tree thieves."

THIRTEEN

Brian Erickson

THE MORNING after the article appeared in the paper, the phone rang while the Quiggs were eating breakfast. Walter got up to answer it.

"That was a Mr. Erickson," he informed the family when he returned. "He's a naturalist at the Roseville Arboretum."

Flora's stomach gave a lurch.

"Seems he got pretty excited when he read the story in the paper about our tree rustlers. He's doin' some kind o' research project on walnut trees and wants to take a look at our grove. I told him to come on out, so he'll be here this afternoon."

He turned to Flora. "How 'bout you bein' Mr. Erickson's guide, Flora? You know the way better'n anybody."

"Sure, I guess so," Flora agreed, though escorting another stranger through the woods was the last thing she wanted to do.

AROUND four o'clock an old yellow Jeep bounced up the driveway, and a young man with tousled red hair jumped out. Watching from the window, Flora saw him pat a brown and white dog in the back seat, then stride toward the porch. When she opened the door, he grinned at her through a mass of freckles.

"Hi, I'm Brian Erickson," he said, extending his hand, "but please, call me Brian. And you must be Flora, the girl who helped the cops capture those tree thieves."

Flora nodded, smiling back. "Come on in and meet my aunt," she said, showing him into the hallway.

"I suppose you're wondering why I'm here," said Brian after Abbie had introduced herself. "Well, you see, I work part time at the arboretum, but I'm also a grad student at the university. Right now I'm studying an acid in the leaves and roots of black walnut trees that leaches into the soil and affects other plants. That's why when I read the story in the paper about the tree poachers, I was so anxious to see your walnut grove and maybe collect some soil samples for my project."

Abbie smiled. "Well, Flora here's the one who can show you the way to the woods. She knows all the trees and flowers by name, and she's even thinkin' about takin' some classes this summer at the . . ."

Flora seized Brian's arm. "We really better go, Aunt Abbie," she broke in. "It kind of looks like rain."

"Take your raincoat then," Abbie advised, grabbing Flora's slicker off the rack and handing it to her. "It was nice meeting you, Brian," she said, waving good-bye. "Good luck with your project!"

As soon as they were outside Flora stuffed her raincoat under the porch. "I think the sun's going to stay out after all," she said a little sheepishly.

Brian didn't seem to notice. He was heading for the Jeep. "Would it be all right with you if my dog comes with us?" he asked.

"Sure, bring him along," said Flora, "I love dogs. My grandmother's dog died last year, and I really miss him." The dog watched them with soulful eyes through the window. "What's his name?"

"Barney," Brian told her. "He's part springer, part mutt—and from the way he can leap through the air, I sometimes wonder if he's part dolphin, too!"

Flora laughed. She was beginning to like Brian in spite of herself. Maybe it was his lopsided smile, or the awkward way he ran his fingers through his hair when he talked.

Brian opened the car door and Barney clambered out, his whole body wriggling with joy. He licked Flora's hand, then fixed his eyes on Brian's face, waiting for a signal that would tell him he was going to be invited along on this jaunt.

"Okay, fella," said Brian, giving the dog a quick pat, "let's go!" And off they went, with Barney bounding along beside the path, snuffing at stumps and burrows as Flora led Brian toward the listening rock. The redbud trees were in bloom and their color floated like soft pink clouds through the green lace of the other trees. Clusters of dogwood blossoms shimmered like stars, transforming the woods into an enchanted forest.

"Look!" cried Flora, stopping to admire a cluster of tall white flowers nodding beside the path. "Sweet cicely!" When she was little she used to imagine fairy brides carrying the tiny blossoms in their wedding bouquets.

"Have you ever smelled a sweet cicely root?" Brian asked her. He pulled up a small plant whose buds hadn't opened and broke off a bit of its long skinny root. He handed it to Flora. "Take a sniff," he told her.

"Licorice!" she said in surprise. "Mmmm," she took another whiff, "I never knew roots had smells."

"The early settlers used this root to flavor cakes and cookies," said Brian, "—and the Indians used it in medicine to heal sore throats. There are lots of wildflowers that were used for both food and healing."

"Some are poisonous, though, aren't they?" Flora asked as they continued on toward the creek.

He nodded. "There's a poisonous one right there," he said, pointing to a white eight-petaled flower with a reddish stem and one large, deeply lobed leaf.

"Bloodroot is *poisonous*?" Flora asked in amazement.

"If you ate the root, it would make you quite sick," he assured her. "The Indians had to learn the hard way which plants were good for them and which to avoid. They taught us a lot about the medicinal uses of herbs and wildflowers, and many of our medicines today contain ingredients from wild plants."

Flora felt herself growing eager to show Brian more of the wonders in these woods. They followed Barney, who had already splashed across the creek and was heading up the bank on the other side.

"I think you have even more varieties of wildflowers in your woods than we do at the arboretum," observed Brian, "— wild ginger, Jacob's ladder, crinkleroot, catchfly. Maybe you'd let me bring some of the other naturalists over here sometime to see them."

Flora felt herself stiffen. Showing Brian around was fun—but she didn't like the idea of anyone else wandering around in here. This was the one place that was still hers alone, and she didn't feel ready to share it with any more strangers.

"Well, it was just a thought," Brian went on when she didn't answer. "You can think about it." Suddenly he stopped and arched backward to stare at the walnut trees looming ahead. "Whooo!" He gave a long, admiring sigh. "Those trees—they're gorgeous! No wonder thieves had their eye on them. The taller ones must be worth a fortune!"

"Really?" Flora stared up at the trees she had passed under so many dozens of times, never considering their worth, only seeing them as a familiar part of her own world. Together they stepped under the towering canopy of walnut trees as if entering a cathedral. The forest floor was a tapestry woven of dark shadows and dappled sunlight. For several moments neither of them spoke, then a warbler hidden in the branches above burst into song.

"It's hard to believe, isn't it," said Brian, "that there are people who'd think nothing of chopping down this whole woods if it meant making some quick money. Greed does strange things to people. Makes them forget there's a future."

"Why are walnut trees so valuable?" Flora asked him.

"Well, for one thing, the wood doesn't split or crack when it's cut," he replied, "so it makes good veneer. That's wood that's sliced thin and bonded onto other wood. Indiana's famous for its beautiful veneer—and for the walnut cabinets and other furniture made from it."

Brian took a set of jars from his backpack and started filling them with soil samples from around the trees. "I'd like to come back and do other tests later on," he told Flora, "but for now, these samples are all I need."

On their way back Barney snuffled through the underbrush, frightening a small garter snake that slithered across the path in front of them. Flora laughed as it brushed the edge of her sneaker and disappeared under a rock.

Brian seemed surprised at her lack of fear. "You really do love these woods, don't you, Flora?"

She shrugged. "They're like home," she replied. "I've been coming here since before I could walk." She held a branch out of the way so it wouldn't lash his face.

"You know, we've got a training class at the arboretum for kids who think they might be interested in becoming naturalists someday," Brian told her. "The class is going to meet every day for three weeks; and when they're finished, the students will help with our other summer workshops—like *Aquatic Insects, Toads and Tadpoles, Forest Survival*. We could really use someone like you, Flora, who's already comfortable in the woods and knows a lot about wildlife. How about joining us? The class starts two weeks from today—just a few days after school's out."

Flora shook her head. "No thanks, I don't think so," she said. "It sounds great and everything, but I'm going to be too busy."

"Oh?" Brian's face brightened with interest. "Doing what?"

Flora stopped to remove a stone from her sneaker. Why did people have to keep pestering her about her plans for the summer? Why couldn't she do what she'd always done—work in the garden, go on picnics by herself, sit in her tree with a good book? It was *her* life. She wanted to make her *own* decisions.

When Flora didn't answer him, Brian said, "If you want, you could just visit the class the first day to see what it's like. Then if you didn't want to come back, that'd be okay. What do you say?"

Flora picked up a stick and threw it as far as she could for Barney to chase. "I'll think about it," she said.

FOURTEEN

Wet Feet

LATER, after Brian had met Uncle Walter and they'd all had lemonade on the porch, Brian finally got up to leave.

"It sure was nice meeting you folks," he told them, shaking their hands again. "And I really appreciate your inviting me back to do some follow-up studies on the soil in your woods." He paused, turning to Flora. "Remember, if you change your mind, Flora, just give me a call at the arboretum. We could sure use your help."

Flora was sure her aunt would question her about Brian's remark after he left, and was surprised when she didn't. All she said was, "I like that young man. I'm glad he'll be coming again so we can get to know him better."

————

TWO DAYS after school was out Flora phoned Brian at the arboretum. "Is there still room for me in the training class?" she asked him.

"I saved you a place," he told her, "in hopes you'd change your mind."

"What time should I be there, and what should I bring?"

"Nine o'clock—and bring binoculars if you have them. And extra socks. You might get your feet wet at the tadpole pond."

"I'm coming just for one day, remember—to try it out," Flora reminded him.

"Right," he replied, "just one day. See you tomorrow."

THE NEXT morning Flora woke to murky skies and rain pattering at the windows. She wondered now why she had changed her mind and told Brian she would come to the class. But she guessed it was too late to back out; she'd promised him she would be there.

After a hurried breakfast Flora pulled on her yellow slicker and black rubber boots and followed Uncle Walter out to the pickup. As soon as they were rolling along the highway he snapped the radio on to listen to his favorite country music station. Twanging guitars mixed with thwapping windshield wipers made conversation impossible, but that was fine with Flora because she didn't feel much like talking.

"You got enough money for bus fare comin' home?" Walter asked her as they pulled into the arboretum parking lot.

Flora nodded.

"Okay then." He reached over and gave her shoulder a shake. "Keep your chin up, okay?"

"Okay." Flora forced a smile and climbed out of the truck. "Thanks for the ride, Uncle Walter."

Standing in the rain, Flora watched until the pickup turned at the end of the driveway and disappeared. Then, with a heavy sigh, she headed for a rustic building with a sign over the door that said Nature Center.

Inside, a group of seven or eight kids (all older than she was, she noted with dismay) were gathered in a pine-paneled room filled with folding chairs. Relief flooded through her when she finally caught sight of Brian in his green uniform. He arranged the chairs in a circle, then asked all the kids to introduce themselves and tell what school they were from. Flora was too nervous to remember any of their names. And when it was her turn to speak, she discovered with horror that she'd completely lost her voice. But nobody laughed. They just sat there, waiting.

Brian came to her rescue. "This is Flora Haywood," he told them, "who lives on a lovely patch of woods south of town. Remember to ask her for help when we're studying wildflowers because she's already an expert."

Oh, great, thought Flora, now they'll think I'm some kind of weirdo. But when she looked up, the girl across the circle was smiling at her.

"Believe it or not," Brian was saying, "some of the children you'll be working with have never been in a woods before. They'll be frightened at first of things that are new to them—things that television and adults who didn't know better have taught them to be afraid of—like worms and snakes and spiders. So our first and most important job is to help children feel safe in the woods."

Brian's words made Flora uncomfortable. She couldn't help remembering all the things she'd told Missy to make her afraid of the woods. If Brian knew all the terrible and untrue things she'd said, he would never have asked her to join this class, she was sure of that.

Because it was raining, the group was given a tour of the Nature Center first, studying displays that would help them identify the trees and flowers and animals they would see later in the woods. After lunch when the sun came out, Brian led the group on their first real tour of the arboretum. They followed trails to places marked on their maps: The Fern Garden, Muskrat Marsh, and the Honeybee Tree where swarms of bees were busily making honey.

Along the trail they passed an ancient maple with bare branches and rotting bark. "We don't clear any dead trees out of these woods," Brian explained, "because eventually they decay and add rich organic matter to the soil. It's nature's own recycling system. The insects that attack the dead wood provide food for woodpeckers and other birds, and this particular tree—because it's hollow inside—is home to a family of raccoons." And as if they had been summoned onstage, two raccoon cubs poked their noses out of a hole halfway up the tree.

Throughout the tour Flora kept to herself, hanging back a little behind the others; but on the final stretch of trail leading back to the Nature Center, the girl in front of her suddenly turned around. "Do you know the name of those lavender flowers over there—" she pointed, "—the ones that smell so sweet?"

"They're phlox," Flora replied. "We have them all over our woods, too."

The girl fell into step beside her. "My name's Simone," she said. "You're the one who knows all the flowers, right?"

Simone was shorter than Flora, with cropped hair and braces. She had a breezy manner that Flora envied.

Flora shook her head. "I only know the ones that grow in my grandmother's woods," she replied. "But I want to know more."

"So do I," said Simone with a burst of enthusiasm. "I love studying about trees and plants and bugs and stuff. My parents think I'm crazy because I practically live outdoors. But I get scared out of my wits when I read about acid rain and toxic waste and forests being cut down right and left. That's why I'm taking this class. I want to learn everything I can so I can become a biologist someday and figure out ways to keep the world from turning into a giant garbage dump."

Flora could hardly believe she was talking to someone her own age who felt the same way she did about the outdoors. She wanted to ask Simone more about herself, but felt too shy. Maybe later in the week, she thought, when they'd known each other longer.

The class's last stop was at the Tadpole Pond. Brian gave each of them a small net attached to a pole and asked them to catch some tadpoles to place in an aquarium for closer examination. Flora wandered along the bank until she spotted some tadpoles swimming close to the water's edge. She positioned her net over the water, swung it down fast, then slipped in the mud and fell—KERPLOP! into the pond.

Simone and Brian dropped their nets and rushed to help her out of the water. While Flora was drying off with a towel from Brian's emergency supply pack, Simone suddenly pointed at her dripping pant leg and burst out laughing. "Hey, Flora," she exclaimed, "that's a pretty tricky way to catch a tadpole!"

Flora looked down. Sure enough, there was a tadpole wriggling in the folds of her rolled-up jeans! For a moment she didn't know whether to laugh or cry. But by the time she had scooped the tadpole out of her cuff and thrown it back in the pond, she, too, was howling with laughter.

FIFTEEN

The Quarrel

"WHAT WOULD you like to do on your birthday?" Abbie asked Flora a few days later as the two of them were finishing up the supper dishes. "The seventh of June is less than two weeks away."

Flora looked up in surprise from the pot she was scrubbing. "How did you know my birthday?"

"Your grandmother left us a letter tellin' us a lot o' things about you," Abbie replied as she dried the last plate and put it in the cupboard.

"What kinds of things?" Flora was shocked to think that Gram had said things about her in a letter to people she hardly knew, even if they were distant relatives.

Abbie hesitated. "Well, mostly she said she loved you very much and wanted us to know what a special person you are." Her face grew thoughtful then, as if she were trying to make up her mind about something. But when she spoke again, all she said was, "You haven't told me yet what you'd like to do on your birthday."

"Nothing special," Flora replied, wondering what it was her aunt wasn't telling her. "I mean, I don't want a party or anything."

She remembered how Gram had always hidden her gifts under a big cloth napkin by her plate at breakfast—and how she always served the orange juice in fancy wine glasses and fixed waffles with real maple syrup. Sometimes they would go to a restaurant for supper, then come back to the house afterward for birthday cake and ice cream. The cake would be angel food with satiny white icing decorated with real pansies or petunias or forget-me-nots. A birthday without Gram would be unbearable. Especially this one. Her twelfth. The year Gram would have given her the china cup that now lay in pieces on her dresser.

Abbie broke into Flora's thoughts. "If we *did* have a party, though," she persisted, "who would you like to invite? Some friends from school—or the arboretum?"

"No! Don't invite anyone!" Seized with panic, Flora pleaded with Abbie. "I don't want a party. I don't want *anything*."

Abbie's smile vanished and her face grew tight. "I declare, I never knew a child so difficult to please!" She whipped her apron off and tossed it in the closet, then crossed her arms and stood facing Flora. "For weeks now—ever since we moved in here, Flora, we've all been tryin' to help you forget your loss. But every time I try to do somethin' for you, you just close me out—or you take off into the woods. The way I see it, bein' by yourself so much isn't natural. It's not good for you."

Flora felt rage rise in her like foam on a kettle of boiling jam. "How can you know what's good for me?" she shrieked at her aunt. "You hardly *know* me. All you want is for me to be like your other kids so I'm not such a misfit. Well, I'm not like them and I never will be. Gram would hate how you've turned this whole house upside-down—and how you keep trying to turn me into something I'm not!" She burst into tears. "I wish you'd never come here—*any* of you!"

When Flora rushed for the door, she found it blocked. Doreen, Curtis, Missy, and Pollyann were all clustered in the doorway staring at her, wide-eyed, while Walter loomed in the shadows behind them. Doreen looked frightened, and Missy was crying.

Abbie hurried over and waved them away. "Go on now," she ordered, "get back to what you were doing. This is between Flora and me. She's wrought up tonight, that's all. She didn't really mean all those things she said."

Slowly they turned and shuffled off to the other room. Flora could hear Walter trying to quiet Missy, murmuring over and over that everything would be all right. A wave of despair washed through her. It wasn't true, she thought. Things were *not* going to be all right. Not now. Not ever.

When Abbie said her name and reached out to touch her, Flora brushed past her and fled to her room. She didn't want anything from Abbie. All she wanted was to be alone.

SOMETHING changed after that quarrel in the kitchen. The Quiggs treated Flora differently. For one thing, they were all very polite and lowered their voices when they spoke to her. They didn't criticize her or make her do things she didn't want to do. It was as if she were a glass figurine teetering at the edge of a shelf, and they were all tiptoeing around her, afraid she might fall.

At first it was okay. Flora didn't mind being ignored: it was a relief. She didn't miss Curtis's snotty remarks or Missy's questions or Abbie's nagging. When she was at the arboretum she didn't think about the Quiggs at all, and the rest of the time she read books in her room or worked in the garden.

Sometimes, though, she caught them looking at her—Missy especially. She would be curled up on her bed reading when something would make her look up—and there would be Missy, leaning against the dresser, staring at her. "Do you want something?" Flora would ask. And Missy would shake her head and run away.

Flora was especially aware of Abbie's distant watchfulness. Whenever her aunt spoke to her, her tone was friendly but guarded; and she didn't pry into Flora's comings and goings the way she used to. Maybe it was just that she was busy and didn't have time to talk. But Flora knew there was more to it than that.

One rainy afternoon when Curtis and Missy were downstairs watching TV and Doreen was off somewhere with her friends, Pollyann toddled into Flora's room lugging a book. Flora was sitting cross-legged on the floor, pressing leaves into a scrapbook, when Polly laid the book on her knee. "Wead?" she asked hopefully, tipping her head to one side.

Flora smiled and lifted the chubby girl onto her lap. "Oh, it's *Millions of Cats*," she exclaimed, opening the book, "—one of my favorites!"

Polly grinned and settled herself comfortably between Flora's knees. Of all the Quiggs, Polly was the only one who seemed unchanged by Flora's outburst in the kitchen. She found a loose corner of Flora's shirt and pulled it up to her mouth along with her thumb. Flora rocked her gently as she read—then at Polly's insistence went back to the beginning of the book and read it again. For a few moments the words of the story and the warmth of Polly's body against her own made her forget the tight, aching place inside her.

But the spell was broken when Abbie marched into the room and snatched Polly up into her arms. "I'm sorry, Flora," she apologized curtly, "I've told her over and over not to come up here botherin' you."

"Fora *wead!*" Polly whimpered, trying to wriggle free of her mother's grasp.

Abbie only gripped her tighter. "It's time for your bath, Pollyann," she said briskly. "I've already got the water runnin'."

"Maybe we can read another story after your bath," Flora said to Polly, who was still thrashing and wailing.

"No, no," Abbie insisted, "I can see you're workin' on somethin' and Polly's interruptin' you. I've told her a hundred times not to come in here, but she doesn't listen."

"But I *want* her to come in," Flora protested. "I like reading to her—*really*."

Abbie didn't seem to hear her. She just hustled Pollyann off down the hall, leaving Flora to her scrapbook and her pile of tumbled leaves.

KEEPING up a pretense of politeness was too much for the Quiggs, and in a few days life was back to normal. Or almost. Doreen couldn't help reminding Flora every now and then that she'd hurt her mother's feelings and ought to be grateful that Abbie was speaking to her at all. And Flora couldn't help noticing that there still seemed to be a kind of invisible wall between herself and her aunt that went up whenever they were in a room together. It made her edgy and sad; but after the awful things she'd said, she didn't know how to make things right between them.

SIXTEEN

Alone

By HER third week at the arboretum, Flora found herself looking forward to what each new day there would bring. Simone waited for her under the sycamore tree by the Nature Center, and they always walked together on the trail hikes. Brian seemed to have an endless supply of surprises for the class, and each day they learned things that made Flora hungry for more.

One day a professor of ornithology from a nearby college spoke to them about birds and took them on a hike to identify the most common species. Another day Brian talked to them about life in prehistoric times and how receding glaciers had made this area of Indiana rich in fossils. All afternoon they had dug in the creek beds, and when Flora found a horn coral fossil she held it up in delight, exclaiming, "A willapus-wallapus toe!" And from that moment on, the fat, pointed fossils were known as willapus-wallapus toes to everyone in the class, including Brian.

When Flora got home that day, she found Curtis hunched in his usual spot on the rug in front of the TV. "Which hand do you want?" she asked, standing in front of him with both hands behind her back.

"Get outa the way, Flora," he growled at her. "Can'tcha see I'm tryin' to watch 'The Munsters'?" He swatted her legs, but she didn't budge.

"Which hand?" she repeated.

"If you think you're connin' me into grabbin' some slimy thing from that nature place, you're nuts," he said, sidling away from her.

"No, c'mon," she urged, "it's not slimy. I promise. Which hand?" she asked again.

Finally curiosity got the better of him and he pointed, lips pursed in disgust.

Flora brought her right fist out from behind her back and dropped something small and heavy into his hand.

"Hey!" he exclaimed when he saw what it was. "A fossil! Where'd ya get it, Flora? Can I keep it?"

And while a rerun of "The Munsters" flickered behind them, Flora told Curtis all about brachiopods and how four million years ago they were swimming around in a glacial sea right on this very spot. Curtis pretended to be bored, but the next day Flora found him with a book on fossils he'd checked out of the library.

After that, she saved all the fossils she found in the creek and deposited them on Curtis's dresser every night, even though she still thought he was an obnoxious twerp.

ON THE seventh of June, a Wednesday, Flora woke with a strange empty feeling in her chest. At first she didn't know what it was. Then suddenly she remembered . . . this was her birthday! She'd hoped the day would slip by without even remembering. But now that she had, nothing could stop the rush of feelings that flooded through her . . . the special plans she had made with Gram . . . the memories.

Missy's bed was empty. Well, *that* was a relief. She wouldn't have to start the day bombarded by a zillion questions. And today was "Bug Day" at the arboretum when Brian would help them identify insects they found in the woods and around the pond. She hoped he'd keep them so busy that she wouldn't have time to remember how today was supposed to be different from all the others.

After dressing in a T-shirt and cutoffs, Flora started for the stairs—but stopped when the red bandanna on her dresser caught her eye. Not once had she touched it since Abbie had handed it to her, lumpy and sharp with pieces of the broken cup inside. She touched it now. Tears sprang to her eyes as she untied the knot, lifted a shard from the pile and held it in her hand. One of the painted violets was still intact, its green leaves and stem curving softly across the ivory surface.

Then, as Flora gazed at the violet, a strange thing happened. The petals began to sway like a reflection on water; and for just a moment, through a blur of tears, Flora saw her grandmother's face smiling up at her. A sob caught in her throat as she cried out, "Gram, it's my birthday!"

The familiar crinkles around her grandmother's eyes deepened. "I know, child, I know," Flora heard her saying. "You have a fine day now, you hear?"

"No!" The word shouted inside Flora's head. "I *won't* have a fine day! Not without you! I don't want to be twelve if you're not here!"

"Child."

Something—a whisper of air from the window?—brushed Flora's cheek. When she touched her hand to the spot, the churning inside her suddenly ceased, and for a moment she was filled with the same peacefulness she always felt when she sat in her tree. "You have a fine day, too, Gram," she whispered. "I love you."

Flora brushed tears from her eyes, still gazing at the piece of broken cup in her hand. Then she put it back with the others and retied the bandanna. Whatever it was that had just happened, she felt no need to understand or question it. Quickly she made her bed and gave her hair a vigorous brushing before heading downstairs.

The kitchen was in its usual chaotic state—TV blaring, Pollyann blowing bubbles in her milk, Missy and Curtis squabbling over a piece of toast, and Abbie circling the table, whapping the air with a fly swatter. In the midst of it all sat Walter, sipping his coffee as calmly as if he were alone on an island. When Flora came in, he smiled at her over the top of his newspaper.

"Mornin', Flora," he said. "Happy birthday!" When she didn't reply, he tipped his head, studying her. "This *is* the day, isn't it?"

Flora nodded. She started to say something, but he raised his hand to stop her. "I know, I know, you don't want us makin' any fuss, and we aren't goin' to. I just wanted you to know we didn't forget." Disappearing again behind his paper he added, "Better eat up now or we'll both be late."

Flora sat down at the table. The carton dripped as she poured milk on her cereal, and she couldn't help remembering how Gram had always put the milk in a blue-and-white flowered pitcher, and how the jam always went into a little round pot with a strawberry on the lid. Abbie had said it was too much trouble to wash those fancy dishes all the time, so she'd put them away where they wouldn't get broken. Flora took a bite of cereal, but couldn't swallow it. Excusing herself from the table, she emptied her bowl into the garbage, washed her dishes, and made a peanut butter sandwich to put in her backpack.

"I'm ready to go now, Uncle Walter," she said.

So what if it was her birthday? Flora argued with herself as she bumped along beside her uncle in the pickup truck. Twelve years old. Big deal. There must be kids all over the world having their twelfth birthdays today. Kids in China. Kids in Africa. Kids in South America. Why should anyone give a hoot about *her* birthday except her?

That gave her an idea. She *would* have a birthday . . . in the woods . . . in her tree. There was no law that said you couldn't celebrate a birthday by yourself. Besides, she wouldn't really be alone. Gram would be there, too. They would celebrate together, just the way they'd planned.

SEVENTEEN

In the Tree

FLORA was glad everyone was busy when she got home from the arboretum that afternoon because it meant she could sneak off to the woods without anyone noticing. She pulled off her muddy clothes, and then on an impulse slipped Gram's embroidered blouse off its hanger and over her head. It fit perfectly. Clean socks, a fresh pair of jeans, and the heartwood box tucked in her pocket. She was ready.

As she passed the open kitchen door she saw a basket of shiny red apples on the table. Suddenly she was hungry and decided to take an apple with her to eat in the tree. Glancing furtively behind her, she slipped into the room and was just reaching toward the bowl when footsteps sounded behind her. She froze.

"Goin' somewhere, Flora?" It was Aunt Abbie, carrying a handful of violets she must have picked at the edge of the woods. "I see you changed your clothes." She smiled approvingly. "Your grandmother's blouse looks pretty on you." She set the flowers in a jar on the sink.

Flora watched her aunt uncertainly. It would be impossible now to sneak off without her suspecting something. She might as well tell her the truth.

"Aunt Abbie," she said, "if it's okay with you, I'd like to go to the woods by myself today—just for a little while. I have this tree on the other side of the creek—and I go there sometimes to be alone. It's not far away. If I shouted good and loud, you could hear me. So I wondered—just this once . . ."

Abbie looked thoughtful. "Sure, I guess it'll be okay," she decided, "just this once. But don't be gone long. It's only an hour till supper."

ONCE she was certain Missy wasn't following her into the woods, Flora relaxed. She was back in her world, and it wrapped her in its quiet beauty. In the three weeks she'd been taking classes, she'd discovered lots of new things about the woods at the arboretum; but this was the woods she would always love best. No patch of woods, she had learned, is quite like any other. Each has its own unique designs and patterns. Each has its own smells and sounds and feelings. And at this time of year, when spring was slipping fast into summer, every day brought wondrous changes. New wildflowers . . . little whiskered faces peering out of burrows and dens . . . and always a changing slant of light across the forest floor.

A Carolina wren warbled from the treetops its "*Tea-kettle, tea-kettle, tea-kettle!*" song. Phlox and daisies and purple vetch spread like a calico quilt under the trees. And even before she could see it, Flora could hear the creek leaping and gurgling with watery laughter.

She had come to rely on these woods to make her feel safe and warm and whole. So why, today, did she have to feel so heavy and cold, as if a stone had been dropped inside her?

Pushing those feelings aside, Flora concentrated on crossing the creek. Up the bank, past the woodpecker tree, around the edge of the walnut grove, and over the ridge to the deserted farmyard. Her tree—fully leafed out now in a glory of shimmering green—waved its arms in welcome. With a running leap, Flora grabbed the lowest branch with both hands and swung herself up into the tree. For a few moments she just sank back against the trunk and closed her eyes, waiting for the heavy feeling inside her to melt away.

After what seemed a long time, when nothing had happened, Flora sat up and opened her eyes. She took the heartwood box out of her pocket and rubbed her finger over the tiny heart as if conjuring up a magic spell. " 'When the time is right,' you said. 'When the time is right. . . .' " A silent tear ran down her cheek. "But you're dead now, Gram, and the time will *never* be right!"

She jammed the box back in her pocket, then yanked out the apple and threw it as hard as she could across the clearing, where it smashed against a tree with a satisfying SPLAT! "I hate these woods!" she screamed at the top of her lungs. "I hate people who die! And most of all, *I hate birthdays!*"

Eventually a pair of nuthatches that had shot out of the tree like rockets at the sound of her screams, returned to their nest. And for a long time Flora sat silently in the tree, staring at nothing. She didn't cry. She didn't feel. It was as if she wasn't even there.

Then at last something made her turn her head; and when

she did, she caught her breath and leaned forward very slowly to make sure she wasn't dreaming. Two deer—a doe and a fawn—were standing right there under her tree, so close she could have reached out and touched them. Where had they come from? she wondered. How could she not have heard them arrive?

The doe raised her head and sniffed the air. Sensing Flora's presence, her long delicate ears pricked forward.

"Don't be afraid," Flora whispered softly. "Stay. Please. I won't hurt you."

For a few moments the deer relaxed and nibbled grass with her fawn. Then again she raised her head and stood motionless . . . alert. As if the fawn were following some silent signal, he, too, raised his head, and the two of them glided in unison, like dancers, across the clearing and back into the shadows of the forest.

Flora scrambled down from the tree and ran fleet as a deer herself down the ridge, through the walnut grove, and along the bank to the creek. *If only I'd brought Missy!* The thought kept repeating itself as she wound over the curving path, dodging briers and catching stray branches with her upraised hand. *If only she'd been with me to see the deer! I have to tell her. I . . . have to . . .*

THEY came at her so fast she didn't have time to think. Something covered her eyes and she staggered backward, unable to see. Someone clutched her shoulders to keep her from falling. Other hands grabbed her, tugging her forward.

What was happening? Who had captured her? And where were they taking her?

EIGHTEEN

A Fine Day

"A FEW more steps, Flora. Just a few more steps."

"Watch out for that hole! There . . . good. Okay, now keep going. We're almost there."

"All right, now *stop!*"

Someone untied the blindfold.

"SURPRISE!"

When she opened her eyes, Flora found herself near the listening rock, surrounded by a circle of Quiggs. Aunt Abbie and Uncle Walter and Doreen and Curtis and Missy and Pollyann were all clapping and jumping up and down, shouting, "Happy Birthday, Flora!" over and over and over. Balloons and streamers hung from the trees, and the listening rock had been magically transformed with a bright blue tablecloth, pink paper plates, birthday napkins, bouquets of daisies, and sprinkles of jellybeans. In the center of the table was an enormous cake swirled with thick white icing and decorated with violets.

Flora blinked back sudden tears. She was so stunned that for a moment all she could do was stare at the table and shake her head. "You did all this . . . for *me?*" she said at last.

"Reaching the ripe old age of twelve calls for a special celebration," Walter declared. "So here we are, ready to celebrate!"

"Can I give her twelve smacks on her rear end?" begged Curtis. He spit on his palms in anticipation.

Walter laid a restraining hand on his shoulder.

"Presents! Presents! Give her the presents!" chanted Missy impatiently. She and Doreen escorted Flora to a log draped with an old quilt and sat her down like a queen on a throne. Abbie and Walter followed, carrying a basket filled with packages. Abbie and Missy sat on either side of her, and the others sat on the ground.

Flora was overwhelmed. "I don't know where to start," she said helplessly.

"Here." Doreen handed her a box from the top of the pile. "It's from me."

Flora slipped off the wrappings and poked through a mound of crinkled-up tissue paper until she found a small plastic case with a mermaid on the cover. She lifted it out and opened it. "Eye shadow?" She peered cautiously at the three circles of color inside, labeled: Iridescent Green, Powerhouse Pink, and Passion Purple.

"I know you don't wear makeup," Doreen explained hurriedly, "but you'll be in junior high next year. You'll need it."

Only on Halloween, Flora thought to herself. But she thanked Doreen and put the case back in the box.

Next she opened a coin purse shaped like a cat from Curtis, a beaded necklace from Pollyann, and from Walter and Abbie a soft green sweater the color of mint.

Missy tapped Flora's arm impatiently. "Don't forget *my* present," she reminded her, plunking a square package from the gift basket into Flora's lap.

Flora grinned as she tugged at the ribbon. "Jellybeans, right?"

Missy tipped her head sideways and gave Flora a mysterious Cheshire cat smile.

Flora pushed back the paper inside the box and lifted out an antique china cup. It was so old that much of the paint had worn off, but a few pink rosebuds were still intact against the ivory background.

"It's not as pretty as the one I broke—" Missy's small brow wrinkled anxiously, "—but I couldn't find one with violets."

"Where *did* you find such an old cup?" Flora turned it around and around in her hands. "It must be as old as Gram's. Maybe older."

Missy grinned proudly. "At a garage sale. Mama stopped to buy some canning jars and I saw the cup and thought you'd like it even if the roses are kind of worn off. The lady let me have it for a quarter because you can see where it broke once and somebody glued it. I hope you don't mind."

Flora ran her finger over the crack. "'Course I don't. Somebody must have loved it a lot to mend it like that." She looked at Missy. "I love it, too."

Now all that was left at the bottom of the basket was a long white envelope. She picked it up and was starting to open it when Walter stopped her. "I'll tell you what's in there so you won't have to take time to read it all now. What it is, is a copy of your grandmother's will, and it says all twenty acres of the woods go to you. The land will be held in trust till you're eighteen, and then you can do whatever you like with it—sell it, build a house on it, even come out here and live in a tree if you've a mind to."

"The whole woods?" Flora was so stunned she could hardly speak. "Gram left me the *whole woods?*"

"Every tree and bush and bumblebee," Abbie replied. "The house she left to us—but furniture, books, everything else in the house'll be yours if you want it."

Flora was so overwhelmed by all that had happened that when she heard a faint "Yip!" behind her, she thought she must be dreaming. Glancing around, all she could see was the listening rock table set for supper. Then she heard it again. "Yip-yip-yip!"

"Didn't you hear that?" she cried, jumping up off the log. "It sounded like a puppy. Maybe it ran away and got lost in the woods."

She dashed into the trees behind the rock and ran smack into a large cardboard box with a huge red bow fastened to one corner. "HAPPY BIRTHDAY TO FLORA, WITH LOVE FROM ABBIE" was written across the front of the box.

Flora looked inside. Now she *knew* she was dreaming! Peering up at her was a ball of grayish fluff with two black eyes and a pink smudge of a nose. "Oh, what a funny little puffball!" she exclaimed, and lifted the pup into her arms.

The puppy scrambled up Flora's chest to lick her chin, making little whimpery sounds against her neck. "Ooo, you're tickling!" she laughed, then held him in front of her to study his face.

The Quiggs hovered around her, chattering excitedly.

"Do you really like him?" Abbie's eyes shone as she watched the two of them getting acquainted.

"Oh, Abbie, I *love* him," Flora exclaimed. "I've been wanting a dog ever since Gram's old collie died last year. But Gram wasn't well enough to take care of a puppy while I was at school, so I just made myself forget it."

"Well, I've been feelin' badly about not lettin' you go to the woods by yourself anymore when you've been doin' it all your life," Abbie told her. "But even bein' on your own property isn't always safe anymore—which we found out the hard way." She reached out to scratch the puppy's head. "But now you'll have a dog to go with you on your walks, and Walter an' me will rest easier knowin' you have some protection."

"O' course, this pooch has some growin' to do before he's good for anything but chasin' his tail," Walter observed with a chuckle. "But the lady at the animal shelter said she could tell from the size of his paws that he's goin' to be a big dog —probably German shepherd size, or even bigger."

"I'll start teaching him things right away," Flora assured them, "and I'll take him to obedience school when he's old enough."

"What are you gonna name him?" Missy asked.

"Dusty," Flora replied without a moment's hesitation, "because he looks just like one of those fuzzy dust balls that roll around under my bed."

They all laughed, agreeing that the name fit him exactly.

When Flora set him on the ground he snuffled around in the leaves, then suddenly took off at a gallop down the path, his ears flapping. "Don't worry, I'll catch him!" cried Missy, and off she went with Curtis and Doreen racing along beside her.

Flora watched them for a moment, then turned to her aunt who had started unpacking one of the picnic baskets. "Aunt Abbie . . . ?" She hesitated, not knowing quite how to begin.

Abbie turned her head. "Yes, hon?" She peered at Flora expectantly.

"I'm sorry for what I said that night in the kitchen . . . I didn't mean it." She stared at the ribbon on Dusty's box, unable to look at her aunt directly. "If you and Uncle Walter hadn't moved into the house, I don't know what would've happened to me. I didn't want things to change . . . and I miss Gram, but . . ." she was having trouble getting the words out ". . . but I'm really glad you're here."

Their eyes met then, and Flora was startled to see that her aunt's were filled with tears. "Oh, Flora," Abbie exclaimed, reaching for Flora's hand, "I'm the one who should be sayin' I'm sorry. Sorry for not listenin' to you . . . for not payin' attention to what you were feelin'. With all the changes you've had to face, you didn't need me addin' more."

Flora dug at the ground with the toe of her shoe. "You think I'm strange, don't you?" she said.

Abbie gave a little gasp. "Why, Flora hon', what's makes you say that?"

"Missy told me. She heard you and Uncle Walter talking one night."

Abbie smiled to herself. "That Missy . . . I shoulda known." She placed her hands on Flora's shoulders and gazed at her steadily. "I did say that," she admitted, "but *strange* can mean a lot o' things."

"I know," said Flora. "Doreen told me I'm strange because I'm *different*. But what she really meant was that I'm *weird*."

"No." Abbie shook her head firmly. "No, you're another

kind of different, Flora. You *know* things—" she looked away, searching for the right words, "—things people don't usually know until they're older. Or things they never know at all."

Flora felt confused. "Like what?" she asked.

Her aunt stared off into the trees for a long time before answering. Then she said, "I know we haven't had time to really get to know each other, Flora, but one thing I do know is that you have a rare kind o' strength in you. A strength that comes partly from your grandmother, I'd guess—but even more from bein' in touch with this world out here—" she waved her arm, "—the earth an' the trees an' the flowers an' all. It gives you a kind of knowin' that—" she hesitated, "—that sets you apart from ordinary folks. It'll burden you sometimes because you'll feel things so deeply. Not just good things either, but hurtin' things, too." A smile came into her eyes then and she brushed Flora's hair away from her face. "This knowin' I'm talkin' about, it's a special kinda gift. While other folks are walkin' around on the earth, missin' things, you'll be swimmin' down deep, seein' it all."

When Flora didn't reply, Abbie arched her eyebrows questioningly. "Did any o' that make sense to you?" she asked, laughing a little.

Smiling back, Flora tipped her head one way, then the other. "A little," she said.

And suddenly they were hugging each other, and crying, and laughing, and hugging again. Then they heard Missy's voice shouting, "We got him!" and the trio of puppy chasers burst out of a thicket into the clearing. "I grabbed Dusty just as he was 'bout to jump in the creek," she said, delivering him triumphantly into Flora's arms.

NINETEEN

Silent Music

It was time now for the birthday supper; and while Flora and Dusty played tug-of-war with a stick, platters of food appeared on the listening rock table as if by magic. There was crunchy fried chicken, fresh fruit salad, potato salad, homemade rolls, and celery sticks stuffed with peanut butter. "Help yourselves, everybody!" called Walter, hustling Flora to the front of the line.

They all heaped their plates, then arranged themselves on blankets spread on the ground. When it was time for the cake, Doreen reminded Flora to make a wish before blowing out the candles. As soon as Flora closed her eyes, she saw again her grandmother's face—heard her saying, *You have a fine day now, child, you hear?*

Flora smiled to herself and opened her eyes. She took a deep breath and blew out all twelve candles at once.

"Hurray! Your wish will come true!" shouted Missy, clapping her hands.

Flora realized then that she hadn't made a wish. But it didn't matter. The only thing that could have made this day any finer would have been having Gram here to share it.

"The first piece of cake is for you, Missy," she said. "Hold out your plate."

WHEN supper was over and the leftover food packed away, Curtis suggested they play a game. "People always play games at birthday parties, right?" he said. "So what'll we do?"

"I know!" piped Missy. "The listening game!" She looked at Flora. Dusty was sound asleep in her lap.

"I don't know—" Flora was hesitant. "I've never played with more than two."

But they were all curious now and insisted she teach them. So she explained the rules while Doreen passed around colored pencils and scraps of paper from her sketch pad.

"Who wins?" Curtis wanted to know. "The one who hears the most sounds?"

Flora had never thought of the game as having a winner, but she thought fast. "The winner will be the one who hears something no one else hears."

"All *right*!" Curtis socked the air with his fist. "Let's go!"

They all found places on the ground and closed their eyes. Sounds that only moments before had been drowned out by talk and laughter became suddenly clear, like stars growing bright when the sky goes dark. Flora let several minutes go by, then—when all the pencils had stopped scribbling—said, "Time's up! Now we compare lists. When it's your turn, name one sound that no one else named, and we'll keep going around the circle until there are no sounds left."

Everyone pulled closer together. "I'll start," said Abbie. She looked at her list. "The first sound I heard was water babbling in the creek."

"Bumblebee buzzing," said Doreen.

"Airplane," said Walter.

"Crow cawing," said Curtis.

Missy was next. She squinted hard at her list. "Woodypecker tapping!" she said with a grin.

"Cricket chirping," Abbie continued.

"Branches creaking."

"Frog croaking."

And on they went until finally everyone had run out of sounds. Everyone except Missy. "I have one more!" she cried, waving her paper in the air.

"She probably made something up," grumbled Curtis, "just so she could win."

"Did *not!*" Missy gave him a fierce look. "I *heard* it."

"Heard what, Missy?" Walter asked her.

Turning suddenly shy, Missy glanced hesitantly around the circle. Then very softly she said, "I heard the earth's heart beating."

A snort of laughter exploded from Curtis. "See what I mean? She's makin' that up." He turned to Missy and gave her a cuff on the head. "The earth doesn't *have* a heart, fleabrain, so how could you hear it?"

Missy lifted her chin. "Well, maybe I didn't hear it, but I *felt* it!"

When Curtis laughed again, Abbie said, "You know, I think I felt it, too. I've never been in a woods before, just listenin' to things like we were doin', but I did sense a faint sort of throbbin' in the air like . . . like silent music.''

Flora had felt that silent music many times—stretched on her back under a pine tree, sitting alone on the creek bank, or just curled up quietly in her tree. She had never tried to describe it in words. It was simply there—the rhythm of the earth— like the steady beating of her own heart.

TWENTY

"When the Time Is Right"

CURTIS had started to wheeze, and Polly was rubbing her eyes, so Abbie decided it was time to pack up and head home.

"Can't we stay longer?" begged Missy. "I like it here."

When Abbie said no, they really must leave, Flora had an idea. "How about if I stay here with Missy for a while?" she suggested. "There's something I want to show her before we go home."

Abbie looked doubtful, then decided to relent. "Well, if you're sure. . . ."

"I'm sure."

"All right then. We'll take Dusty back with us." She gave Missy a pat on her backside. "Be back before dark now, both of you!"

"WHAT do you want to show me?" Missy asked when she and Flora were alone.

"It's a surprise," said Flora. "Just follow me across the creek, and try not to fall in."

As they started up the path on the other side, Missy hung back, peering with suspicion at the dense clump of trees ahead. "I don't wanna go in there," she said. "I'm afraid."

"In where?"

Missy pointed. "There. Where the blumps are."

"We won't go near any blumps," Flora promised. "Just follow me. It'll be okay."

Missy kept walking, but her steps were cautious. "I brought jellybeans for the willapus-wallapus," she announced loudly, as if she hoped the willapus-wallapus might hear her. "Purple ones, so he won't eat us up."

Flora didn't answer. She hated herself for creating so much fear in Missy. Maybe now would be a good time to set things straight.

"Missy, remember when we saw those white blobs on that old stump, and . . . *Missy, don't touch that!*"

With a yelp of fear, Missy jumped back, clutching her jellybean sack to her chest.

Flora put her hands on Missy's shoulders. "I'm sorry I scared you," she said, "but you were about to touch poison ivy. See those plants with three shiny green leaves?" Missy nodded, her eyes still wide with fright. "Well, if you touch them, you could get a rash that itches like fury. But you don't need to be afraid of poison ivy," she hastened to add. "Now that you know what it looks like, you can just stay away from it."

"But what if it doesn't stay away from *me*?" Missy wailed.

"Well, if you touch some by mistake, then just wash with

soap as soon as you can. And always wear socks and long pants when you hike in the woods."

"Can I wash blump juice off, too?" Missy asked, still trembling a little.

"Missy—" Flora's words came slowly, "I made up all that junk about blumps. I wanted to scare you so you wouldn't follow me into the woods all the time. Those white blobs I showed you are really bracket mushrooms. And they won't hurt you a bit if you touch them."

She was about to tell her she'd made up the willapus-wallapus, too, but the hurt and confusion on Missy's face made her stop. The willapus-wallapus was different from the blumps. She couldn't just tell Missy it didn't exist because . . . well, in a way it *did* exist, and she'd become . . . well, *fond* of it. They both had. She couldn't destroy it. It wouldn't be right.

"Maybe you'd like to take one of the workshops I'll be helping with at the arboretum," Flora suggested as they picked up their pace. "There's one on moths and butterflies starting next week."

"Butterflies?" Missy's face brightened. "I love butterflies! Once when I was sitting in the grass a yellow butterfly came and sat on my knee. She kept opening and closing her wings like she wanted me to see how pretty she was. I named her Lilyann Angelina."

And the memory of Lilyann Angelina led to a barrage of questions that ordinarily would have had Flora reeling: "What do butterflies eat?" "Where are their eyes?" "What are their wings made of?" "Where do they go in the winter?"

But this time Flora answered patiently and was surprised to discover that she enjoyed sharing what she'd learned in the arboretum class. And it occurred to her when she saw the eager glow on Missy's face that Missy had never meant to annoy anyone with her questions. She had a passion for learning things, that's all, just as Flora had a passion for trees and birds and other living things. Missy *needed* to ask questions, and she needed honest answers. It would be fun to have her in the butterfly class.

Soon the two of them were scrambling up the same embankment Flora had tried to stop Missy from climbing a few weeks before.

"You sure you want me here?" Missy asked when she realized where they were.

Flora reached for Missy's hand. "Come on," she said, "I'm going to take you to my tree."

Missy frowned. "Your hugging tree?"

Flora laughed. "Don't look so worried. I won't yell at you this time, I promise."

Missy walked around and around the tree, patting the bark and gazing up into the branches.

"Here, I'll give you a boost." Flora grasped Missy around the waist and hoisted her to the first branch.

"Ooo, this is nice!" Missy nestled into the V where the trunk met the branches. "I'm a squirrel!" she squeaked. "No, I'm an owl! *Whooo! Whooo!*"

Flora sat on the branch next to her, dangling her legs in the warm evening air. For a while the two of them just sat there together, watching the sun sink like a giant peach into a crimson sea. Crickets chirred and peepers trilled, lulling the forest to sleep.

"Just think, Flora," remarked Missy, snuggling even deeper into the arms of the tree, "this whole woods belongs to you now. You're Queen of the Forest!"

Flora shook her head. "That may be what it says on some piece of paper, but I don't think land can belong to anyone. Land and people belong to each other."

"What do you mean?"

"Well . . ." she thought a moment, "people are born and live and die, but the land is here forever. So how can people own it? All they can do is love it and take care of it for whoever comes along next. Besides," she added, "the woods are my only family now. And the best thing about that is that they'll never leave me."

"But we're your family, too," Missy insisted, "and we won't leave you—*ever!*"

Deep down—in spite of all the reservations she had about the Quiggs—Flora knew what Missy said was true. Abbie and Walter would never desert her. Of course, no one would ever take Gram's place—and the Quiggs *were* going to take a lot of getting used to. But in a peculiar way they seemed to need her—and hard as it was to believe, maybe she needed them too.

"When I was here earlier," she told Missy, "two deer came and stood right under this tree—a doe and a fawn. They were so close I could have touched them. That's what I was coming to tell you when you and Curtis and Doreen tackled me by the creek."

"Do you think they'll come back," Missy asked breathlessly, "—while we're still here?"

"Maybe," said Flora, "but we can't stay any longer tonight. The sun's going down, and I promised I'd have you home before dark."

———

As THEY passed through the walnut grove on their way home, Missy stopped to peer up into the leafy canopy over their heads. "Look, Flora!" she exclaimed. "The branches have hands!"

Flora looked up. Sure enough, the new green leaves did look like skinny hands with long pointed fingers.

Many fingers on each hand. The words drifted through her mind. She wondered why they sounded so familiar . . . and then she remembered. The riddle! Suddenly her insides were churning with excitement. "Missy, listen," she told her. "Do you remember this?" And she recited: " 'Tall, dark, handsome; straight they stand; many fingers on each hand.' "

For a moment Missy looked puzzled. Then her face lit up. "Your grandmother's riddle!"

Flora went on: " 'Gifts they carry, sweet and small, in chests that swing and sway, then fall.' " She let out a whoop. "Walnut trees have nuts that grow inside round hulls—like little chests!" Her voice rose with excitement. " 'Guard them well, and love them, too—for treasure they will bring to you.' "

"You mean the treasure is walnuts, not *gold*? Phooey!" Missy's face fell. "I don't even like walnuts."

Flora laughed. "No, Missy, it's the *trees*. The trees are the treasure. Remember the tree that got chopped down? The thieves wanted it because it was worth a lot of money—thousands of dollars. Since Gram didn't have any money to leave me in her will, she left me trees instead." Flora threw her arms in the air. "I'm rich!" she shouted. "I'm a millionaire!"

Missy watched her solemnly. "Are you really going to chop down all these trees to get money?"

"Of course not!" Flora answered indignantly. "I'll not cut a single one, even if I'm in the poorhouse."

"Then you're *not* rich," said Missy, relieved and disappointed at the same time. "And you're not a millionaire either."

"Of course I'm not a millionaire, goofus," Flora declared, "but I *am* rich." She tipped her head back again to watch the many-fingered leaves drift and shimmer against the sky. She'd meant it when she said she would never cut down a single tree. She would guard them and love them, just like the riddle said.

"WHEN will I get to see the deer, do you think?" Missy asked when they'd crossed the creek and were back at the listening rock.

"As soon as you learn to be quiet for more than two seconds," said Flora.

"I can be quiet." And the words were scarcely out of her mouth when she gave such a shriek that every leaf in the forest trembled.

"Honest to Pete, Missy, what is it now?"

Holding her arms out stiffly at her sides, Missy stared down at her stomach, blowing and blowing at something that at first Flora couldn't even see. "It's coming up!" she yelped between puffs. "Get it off me, Flora! Get it *off!*"

Very gently Flora seized the daddy longlegs by one leg and lifted him off Missy's shirt. Placing him on her bare arm, she watched as he pawed the air with one threadlike leg.

"Ooogh, Flora, how can you *do* that?" Missy pressed her knuckles hard against her mouth. "He's so prickly-ickly! Aren't you scared he'll *bite* you?"

"Daddy longlegs don't bite," Flora said, studying the spider as he slowly raised one skinny leg and then another on his journey from her wrist to her elbow. "They eat other insects —mostly dead ones—and they're perfectly harmless."

"Well, I don't like them crawling on me. I don't want *anything* crawling on me! I'm never coming to the woods again! Never never never!"

Flora smiled a quiet little smile, remembering how—just a few weeks ago—she had tried to frighten Missy into saying those very words.

"You mean you're not coming with me tomorrow night to wait for the deer?"

"Unh-unh."

"Or play the listening game?"

"Nope."

"Or be a ferny plume?"

"Well . . ." Missy tilted her head. "Do you really think the deer will come back?"

"They might."

For a long moment Missy was quiet. "Okay then. I'll come."

"I'm glad," said Flora. "Deer watching is much better with two."

Then they hooked arms and headed home through the rosy shadows of a soft June twilight.